THEY RUN

THE DIRECTOR

--- PULLING THREADS ---

Book Four

SHERYLL O'BRIEN

ISBN 978-1-939351-06-7

WOODWIND PRESS

Printed in United States of America

Mom,

I love that you love Rocco Fiancetti ---
because he makes you swoon
and he makes you laugh.

ACKNOWLEDGMENT

To those who I have lost along the way.

A heartfelt thank you to my team:

Andria Flores ~ Editor extraordinaire.
Nancy Pendleton ~ Goddess of the publishing world.
Jessica Champion ~ Web designer and manager.
25 Hours Consulting
Daryl Bruinsma ~ Cover Design & Animation.

Testimonials

"One book will set the hook!" ~ Nancy Pendleton

"This avid reader predicts that Sheryll O'Brien will become your favorite author. She's mine." ~ Ruth S. Bodreau

"The characters draw you in immediately. You will worry, laugh, hope, and love right along with them." ~ Donna Eaton

"There is nothing sweeter than a Sunday morning coffee, a blanket, overcast skies, and a *Pulling Threads* novel." ~ Andria Flores

"Everything you'd want in a good book. Humor, romance, suspense and great characters! It even takes place by the ocean! Loved it." ~ Helena Green

"I could write a book about the wonderfulness of it all." ~ Faith

"Hunks, humor, and heartache! What more could you ask for?" ~ Marjorie McCarthy

"*Bullet Bungalow* is a page turning family saga and then *Netti Barn* and *Cutters Cove* come along and add a whole lot of trauma to the drama." ~ Jessica O'Brien

"The most promising new author I've encountered in my publishing career!" ~ Jim P. - Woodwind Press

--- Pulling Threads ---

Bullet Bungalow
Netti Barn
Cutters Cove
They Run
They Hide
They Choose

Coming soon...

PENOBSCOT BAY
A Rocco Fiancetti Incorporated Investigation

Reasons
Rescues
Resolutions
Torment
Tango
Tests
Resolve
Revenge
Rebound

--- Twisted Threads ---

Coming soon...

Her Scream
Stay Safe

Before he knows.
August

John Maxwell was more than halfway through his 12-hour flight from Seattle to Paris. The Mach-speeding tin can in which he sat shimmied and shook, then banged his whiskey over the sides of his glass. He lifted his now-empty tumbler and tilted it from side to side at the first airborne waitress he saw, then wiped his whiskey-wet hand across his whiskey-wet jeans.

The waitress smiled and nodded.

He smirked—he thought. *He was a bit lit*—he thought.

Long-Lean-Lovely sauntered his way. "Mr. Maxwell, cocktail service is suspended until we get through this bit of turbulence."

"This bit of turbulence is responsible for my being without a cocktail and more to the point it's why I want another inebriant."

The very lovely flight attendant smiled. "Yes, Mr. Maxwell, it's a bit of a bumpy ride." She eyed the exceedingly handsome traveler, "You look as though you can handle a bumpy ride." She smiled and bent low. "As soon as the captain turns off the Fasten Seatbelt sign, I will bring your inebriant and whatever else you'd like, Mr. Maxwell." She winked—the tips of her fingers ran along his forearm and hand.

John watched the willowy, ginger-blonde, emerald-eyed, "sure thing" sashay away. *She moves like Roni*, he thought. *She sounds like Joy*, he tried not to think. The first-class passenger reclined and willed himself to sleep.
Big mistake…

"Move," the spitfire young woman with cropped blonde hair and piercing blue eyes demanded as she approached him at his computer terminal. He laughed. "I'm not having the baby," she said when she walked into their dorm room holding a pregnancy test. He did not laugh. "You can't force me to have a baby," she said as she walked out on him. He threatened that he would.

The dead woman taunted him from the grave. "I was Joy Ann Watts. I was Dead On Assignment. I was DOA. I was a ghost. I had no value to them. You betrayed me. I took an assassin's bullet. Now I **am** a ghost."

He startled awake.

They Run

I knew you'd come.

FICA Special Agent, John Maxwell, is on vacation in Nice, France. He is hoping DEA Special Agent, Veronica Shields, will accept his offer to join him. After three days of radio silence from Roni, solitary walks along the French Riviera, and sleeping alone in his hotel bed, he finds himself at a sidewalk café wondering what the hell he is doing in France. At the moment, he knows what he is doing. He is torturing himself with the last words he said to Roni.

"I'm at a place in my life where I know what I want, or more precisely what I don't want. I don't want temporary or look me up when you're in town…"

He shakes his head at the memory. He knows full well that he's only ever been good at temporary. Sure, he's been in a relationship of sorts with Kitt Mahoney since he was fifteen years old, but he's lied to her for most of their time together. He was in love with Joy Ann Watts for fifteen years, but spent little more than a thousand days of that time with her. The last few of them, on the receiving end of her contempt. Deservedly so. The dispirited man is just about to leave the café, perhaps Nice, when he feels a touch on his shoulder.

"I knew you'd come."

John turns toward the woman's voice and locks onto the piercing blue eyes of a ghost named Joy Ann Watts. The beautiful woman standing within reach of his embrace might be on vacation with him—if she wasn't already dead. He tries to quell the tremble in his hand as he tosses francs on the café table. The ghost vanished after speaking a few words—left before the dumbfounded man got his shit together. Had John not felt Joy's hand on his shoulder and the lingering warmth of her touch, he'd think she'd been a hallucination.

"I knew you'd come." Joy's words bang back and forth in his head along with the impotent questions he asked. "How? ... Why?"

"I'm being watched. I can't stay."

Special Agent, John Maxwell, let Special Agent, Joy Ann Watts, leave. The Agent shouldn't have stopped another Agent from leaving, but the man should have stopped the woman. He is on the move now, following along cobblestone streets in search of a ghost he won't find—unless she wants to be found. The fleeting moment with the apparition left him only one clue to follow. He repeats it to himself for fear he'll forget. "She's wearing a full-brimmed straw hat, yellow tank, army-green cargo pants, and strappy sandals. Her hair, or wig, is black; her skin is tanned." He glances at every woman he passes. It doesn't matter if the stranger wears a full-brimmed straw hat with black hair tucked beneath or walks in strappy sandals. Every woman is Joy, or she could be. He knows the description he repeats as a mantra is useless. If the super-spy thinks she is being watched, she will change her look as soon as she meets him, touches him, leaves him. The only thing that won't change is the tortured look in her eyes.

He increases his pace, easily separating out tourists from residents along the seaside village. "Their attire is similar, their movements are different." The Special Agent analyzes the earlier encounter with the ghost. "She presented herself as a tourist. That isn't happenstance, it's a clue. She wants me to think about tourist Joy. I was with tourist Joy every August. It's August," he mumbles, suddenly aware that people pause when they think he is addressing them. He offers nothing and continues on his way. John Maxwell's search for Joy Ann Watts soon takes him down memory lane…

A is for Athens

He fingered the short, wet strands of her hair, lifting a fruity smell that found its way to that place inside him. "Welcome to Athens," he softly growled.

"We've been here for twelve hours. You've ravaged me, showered me, and uttered that phrase three times, already. I would really like to explore things outside of this room." She made a move to get out of bed. He pulled her back. She elbowed him hard and made her escape. "While you explore the Acropolis, I'll be meandering the cobblestones of Plaka."

B is for Berlin

She stepped toward the shower door, his hand sliding down her wet back. "Have fun at the zoo," she called over her shoulder. "I'm off to Tiergarten."

"It's called the Berlin Zoological Garden for a reason, Joy. You could commune with foliage, ponds, and rivers there, while I hang with the animals. We could actually spend time together on this reunion."

"I'm good, thanks."

C is for Calgary

From the jacuzzi tub for two, on the balcony of their hotel room, he suggested they visit the observation deck at the tower that loomed in the distance. He received the answer he expected.

"Nope, but you could come with me to Heritage Park and hang out on the banks of the Glenmore Reservoir."

"Nope." He growled, partly because he wanted her like no other, partly because she wanted him in small increments, but mostly because they'd be going their separate ways, and doing their own things. Again.

"Off the beaten path and outdoors is where she'll be." The super-spy begins his search in Vieille Ville, known by tourists and locals as Old Town. The vibrant but quaint area with narrow cobblestone alleyways and pastel-hued buildings was one of Joy's selections for the alphabetical list they collaborated on so many years ago.

"It's your turn, Joy. Pull a letter."
"N is for Nice!"
"Why Nice?"
"It sounds Neeeece."
She laughed. He smirked and put his hand on their baby bump.

The lone wanderer begins his search from Castle Hill, an idyllic natural wonder of greenery and rushing waterfalls that overlooks the Nice coastline. He spends time at the spacious boulevards of Place Masséna and Promenade du Paillon; lunches at Cours Saleya where he watches for Joy amongst shoppers and pedestrians; walks aimlessly through an olive grove with 100-year-old trees. He no sooner finishes the loop when he starts it again, adding a stroll along the Promenade, a beautiful seaside road that curves around the Bay of Angels beaches. He rests amongst swishing palm trees and ambles through gardens that rival the imagination of an Old Masters painting, hoping to catch a glimpse of Joy.

Darkness ushers a weary John Maxwell to his hotel late that night. He is in desperate need of room service, a hot shower, and a long night's sleep. He will get none of those things. What he gets instead is a request that's been slipped under his hotel room door.

find out who unmasked me –
find out who is after me

Did I know?

The agitated and unrested man is shaking his head as his hotel room door slams shut behind him the next morning. He mutters as he walks the corridor to the stairwell, "I had no clue how I'd spend my time in Nice, but I sure as hell didn't think I'd spend it looking for a dead woman." He slams out of the lobby, his eyes slow to adjust to the bright sun, his mind unable to shake the chaos of the mounting questions. "Dammit, Joy, where the hell have you been for nearly a year? Why didn't you contact me in the States? Why did you approach me here?" He shakes his head at the absurdity of the situation. "I'm here when there is no reason for me to be here. Joy is here, and she had to come back from the dead to be here. I need to find out how the fuck that happened." He gives another shake of his head and admits, "In order to do that, I need to leave Nice." Joy's words come pushing back. "I'm being watched. I can't stay."

He runs his hand roughly through his hair, "If she is being watched, then I'm being watched." For the next two days, John Maxwell goes where Joy Ann Watts would never go: museums, historical sites, architectural wonders. A tall, black, hippy-dude with long dreads, follows along. "Yeup, I've got a tail." On his last day in France, John stays close to *their* café in Old Town. He ambles the narrow alleyways, welcoming the memories of the Augusts they shared—surprisingly, those memories soothe his aching heart, until they bruise it all over again, "Joy. Where are you?"

All sense of urgency and expectation is long gone. He knows he won't find the woman he loved and lost—at least not here. As the waning light of day settles, he takes a seat at their café. He closes his eyes and breathes deeply. He feels her presence. He has always been able to feel her.

"Is that why I never went to your grave? Did I know?"

Now you know.

The unsettled and lonely woman knew it was risky approaching John at the café. As far as he knew, as far as the world knows, Joy Ann Watts is dead and buried in a small cemetery in Laurel Falls, Massachusetts, having been felled by an assassin's bullet. At the time of her "death" she was really pissed at John Maxwell. She tears at the memory of his words—the ones that gutted her.

"I didn't tell them it was Annie who did it—I **had** to protect her. The cold hard fact is this, FICA circled their wagons around me because I am more valuable to them. And I let them do it because Annie is…"

Joy swallows the pain those words cause, and mumbles the things she would have told John had she been able to stay at the café. "I am in danger. You need to figure out what's going on, because if you don't, The Body will find me, and take me. Again."

The former Special Agent is sitting at a bistro table on a rooftop garden terrace, about to do the thing she's tried to do for months, reconcile the events of the past year—the shooting, the imprisonment, the running for her life. She is denied that opportunity by the muffled sound of John's voice. Her heart beats wildly as she scans the space around her. She moves to the edge of the terrace and peers over a tiny, black iron railing. "John," she whispers when she finds him sitting at *their* café. She brushes away tears of loneliness, then gazes at the man who betrayed her—the man who came to Nice—even though he thought she was dead.

"I'm glad you came, John. Now you know."

Déjà vu, all over again.

DEA Special Agent, Veronica Shields, is standing at a massive window overlooking Puget Sound. She isn't daydreaming, she is processing. It's a habit she picked up from her ex-husband, Detective Fred Serpico. The man who walked away from their marriage.

"You or my job. That's it? You're giving me no other options?"

"No."

"Seriously, that's it? This is where we are, Serp?"

"This is where I am, Roni. I don't want to do this. I can't do this."

"What's changed?"

"I've changed, the problem is that you haven't." Fred closed the physical space between them, took her hands in his, "Roni, the field work, you're addicted to it. You don't have to be onsite for the raids, but you can't not be there—you can't stay away from the pits of Hell. The laws of averages say you aren't gonna come home one day. I don't want to be here when the knock comes."

"Serp, I could say the same about you and your job."

"You could, but we both know it's a false equivalency."

"So, you'd rather be alone?"

"No, Roni, I don't want to be alone. I don't want to be without you, but…"

"But we can only be together if I give it all up, if I choose you."

"Yes."

Roni pulled her hands away, ran one through her cropped hair. Her light green eyes showed her anguish, her words cut through it, "I want you, Serp, but I…"

"—choose the job," he finished her sentence.

"Yes."

Fred Serpico left Veronica Shields that night. The instant she heard the door close behind him, she begged the universe, "Please have him ask again. I'll choose him. Please."

He didn't ask again.

It has been two years since the anguished woman let her man walk away, and into the arms of Kitt Mahoney.

Veronica Shields is the senior-most Special Agent in the state of Washington. She is an Agency woman through and through and has an exemplary record. She wouldn't if her higher-ups knew that she broke protocol with a Dead On Assignment FICA agent by maintaining a secret friendship. That infringement would have resulted in disciplinary action for both agents—if they had been found out. Little did they know, they were found out, but the person who knew wasn't ready to play that hand, yet. There are other people who know now. Roni fessed up to two Mayflower-Falls detectives and a FICA Special Agent during the "save Tess, save Annie" case.

"When Joy went Dead On Assignment, she was supposed to end all of her relationships, except for the one she had with John Maxwell. We knew we were breaking DEA and FICA protocol by maintaining a friendship, but she did it because she found her life very isolating. Female agents, even those who aren't Dead On Assignment, have difficulties with relationships because there are so many things that can't be shared or discussed. Almost exclusively, our relationship was personal, and the cornerstone of it was complete honesty."

"Complete honesty," she huffs, then condemns herself, "you wouldn't know honesty if it bit you in the ass. You weren't honest with Fred, and you certainly haven't been honest with John." FICA Special Agent, John Maxwell, has been sharing Roni's life and her bed for nearly a year. He recently gave her an ultimatum: commit to giving their relationship a real try, or go their separate ways. "Déjà vu, all over again," she scoffs. The truth of the matter is this—Veronica Shields might have made a commitment to her relationship with John, but he made the mistake of inviting her to join him on his vacation in Nice. "That's where he and Joy should be, not where he and I should be." Even though Roni desperately wants to be with John, she can't, "Not while he is in Nice with a ghost."

Nice, France

Joy Ann Watts spent considerably more than a decade Dead On Assignment for FICA. It is said that she was so deep undercover that there wasn't air where she worked. Still, the spy made associations with intelligence operatives from across the globe. She never met any of them, but when an agent is in trouble, there is help— even if the agent is "dead". As necessity dictates, the cyber huntress reaches out to a select few undercovers. She trusts them with her life, a surprising state of affairs given the betrayals of the man she trusted above all others. Madame Oosa, a former agent with the General Directorate for External Security, France's intelligence agency, tops the list of operatives Joy trusts. That is why she has been hiding at Oosa's place—that is about to change. Just past daybreak, the owner and operator of the hostel knocks on Joy's door.

"Your man checked out of the hotel last night and is leaving Nice in an hour."

"That means that I'm leaving Nice, as soon as..."

"You get back from John's hotel."

Joy offers a small smile.

"I'll have your things ready when you get back. Joy, I know you want to get one last look at John before he leaves France, but don't forget the danger that follows you."

Joy touches the Madame's arm. "Thank you for your help."

"I'll say my farewells now. Be well, Joy, and when the time comes be in touch. Oui?"

"Oui."

The curly-haired brunette exits from the back of the hostel, follows a narrow cobblestone alleyway to a wide pedestrian walkway, jogs the length of it, heading toward Nice Cathedral. She takes a seat at a café across from Hotel Rossetti, a quaint salmon-colored sandstone structure with white and aqua shutters, and outdoor garden patio with white iron tables and chairs. John is sitting at a corner table having a morning coffee and croissant reading a newspaper.

Joy smiles at the image, remembers back to their choosing Rossetti.

"You know the rules, John. Whoever chose the alphabetical reunion location, chooses the accommodations. What are your objections, and be specific."

"It's quaint."

"It's quiet."

"It's bed and breakfast-y."

"That's not a word, and it's modern luxury inside."

"It's…"

"Settled is what it is."

On two occasions since Joy parked herself at the café, John stopped reading and scanned his surroundings. He felt her presence. He forced himself to not overtly look for her, to not give any indication that she might be near— just in case the hippy-dude was nearby watching him.

As his final hour in Nice nears its end, John alternates between checking his watch and reading his paper. He stays until the very last minute, leaving only after taking one last casual look around. He notices that a curly-haired brunette is no longer sitting at the café across the way, the one who caught his eye, the one he thought might be…

"Joy," he whispers.

After seeing John at Hotel Rossetti, Joy returns to the hostel. She is handed a package as she moves through the lobby, one she doesn't need to inspect, she knows it will contain a new identification packet, and $2,000 cash. Joy sprints to her room, grabs her always-packed duffle, and tosses it onto the bed. From it she removes the ID she used in Nice and destroys it. She reads the name on her new passport, puts it and the cash into the duffle alongside the supplies and provisions she regularly stocks up on. She flips through a stack of travel brochures she picked up at the local agency, pulls one, and reads the name at the top, "Saint Tropez." She tosses the unselected brochures into the trash, takes one final look around, and closes the door behind her. She pulls a deep breath. As she exhales it, she releases a part of her past with John, the N on their alphabetical reunion list.

Take a seat.

Special Agent, John Maxwell, boards a Paris to Boston flight after twisting in the wind for seven days in Nice. He tosses his carry-on into the overhead compartment and his ass onto his seat. He's anxious to get back to the States so he can start working Joy's directive.

**find out who unmasked me –
find out who is after me**

As soon as the Boeing is airborne, he motions to an Uma Thurman lookalike flight attendant.

"Oui, Mr. Maxwell?" she smiles.

"I'd like a cocktail," he smiles.

"We are just about to serve breakfast."

"Great. I'll have whiskey for breakfast."

"Oui, Mr. Maxwell," she smiles wider.

Sex-In-A-Uniform is back within a minute. She hands the first-class passenger a whiskey neat, a cocktail napkin, and a business card that she pulls from between her breasts. "Has anyone ever told you that you look like Aaron Rodgers?" she asks casually.

"You know American football players?" John asks with raised brow.

"Only the cute ones," she replies with a wink.

He smirks. "To answer your previous question, my wife, my mistress, and my three daughters have mentioned the resemblance." The Aaron Rodgers doppelganger leans forward. The Uma Thurman doppelganger leans low. He slips the business card between her breasts. "Darlin', I appreciate the offer, but I've got more woman trouble than I can handle at the moment. Keep the drinks coming, and bring them in nip form."

Uma shrugs her shoulder. "But of course, Mr. Maxwell."

Several hours later, Sex-In-A-Uniform tries one last time. She hands John her business card as he walks past to deplane. "In case you change your mind, Mr. Maxwell. I'm in Boston on a 48-hour layover."

John smiles and pockets the card. He loses his smile when he steps from the passenger bridge and is approached by four J. Edgar Hoover cookie-cutter clones.

"Special Agent Maxwell, come with us," crew cut #1 says.

John casually strolls the concourse flanked by four men in crisp white button-down shirts, black suits, and ear plug mics. No words are spoken as they crisscross the airport terminal. They eventually arrive at a door where four indistinguishable agents stand sentry.

"Special Agent Maxwell, please hand us your weapons and cell phone."

"Why would I do that, Agent?" John asks.

"Security reasons, sir."

"Whose security, Agent?"

The door at which they have been standing opens. FICA Director, Roland Gaffney, fills the doorway. "I want you unarmed, Special Agent Maxwell. I believe you might shoot me when I tell you a story."

The Director waits for John to remove his guns from his shoulder and ankle holster and hand them to crew cut #1.

"Good. Now come in, John."

The tired, pissed, and moderately buzzed Special Agent enters a huge conference room and looks around. A highly polished cherry conference table with twenty burgundy leather chairs flanked around it cuts a good swath of the room. Two very long burgundy couches and a highly polished cherry and brass cocktail bar swaths even more. Set on the table is a single file folder with the dark gray FICA insignia embossed on it. "Big room for just the two of us, Roland."

The Director clears his throat. "You should address me as Director for this meeting, Special Agent Maxwell."

John nods. "Big room for just the two of us, Director."

Roland Gaffney wastes no time getting started. "Special Agent Maxwell, how was your trip?"

"Interesting, Director."

"Yes. Yes. Interesting." There is a long pause before the Director begins again. "You were with Joy." It wasn't a question.

He addressed her as Joy, not as Special Agent Watts, or DOA. John pauses several seconds. "Joy said she was being watched. One of your agents, I presume?"

"Yes. Take a seat, John. There's a lot you don't know. When I'm done explaining this situation, I will answer whatever questions I can. After that, I'm going to give you an assignment. If you refuse the assignment, you will be released from FICA and unable to work for any other federal agency."

John takes a seat.

"Approximately ten months ago, FICA Special Agent, Joy Ann Watts, was shot and critically injured by a cybermenace known as Hector..."

"And died," John interrupts the Director, something he wouldn't do under normal circumstances, but these are not normal circumstances.

The Director contemplates John's words.

John stares at the Director. "Joy Ann Watts was shot and critically injured **and died**. You forgot the **and died** part, Director."

"You get three insubordinate remarks during this conversation. That's number one," John's superior warns. The Director takes a steely breath and starts again. "Joy was never taken to Mayflower-Falls Regional Medical Center after the shooting at Netti Barn. She was taken by ambulance to a small airstrip outside of Laurel Falls and airlifted to a secure medical facility. Approximately one hour before the shooting, Special Agent Watts crashed her FICA systems as is standard operating procedure when a covert agent is unmasked. When I was alerted to DOA's system crash, I put agents in the field to find her and bring her in for her protection. When they got to her, protection was secondary to saving her life. Emergency responders on scene at Netti Barn were medically trained agents. They worked on her in the ambulance and during the med-flight—they worked their asses off." He stops. He stares. He shakes his head. "Joy was critically wounded. The downward trajectory of Hector's bullet struck her in the back. It caused damage to her right lung, part of her liver, and left kidney. She barely made it through surgery."

John is barely making it through this conversation. "You were at the secure medical facility." It wasn't a question.

The Director nods.

John's voice bellows. "My 15-year-old daughter, Joy's daughter, attended the funeral of the mother she never met, a mother who isn't even dead! She sits at her mother's grave every day for hours at a time, a grave from where she was nearly kidnapped by a drug syndicate headed by Paulo Montoya. God damn it, Roland!" John stands from his chair and slams his hand on the table.

The Director remains seated. "That's number two. **Take your seat, Maxwell.**"

John takes his seat.

The Director slides the lone file that's been front and center toward John. While he reads it, the Director moves to the stocked bar at the back of the room. He grabs two Old Fashioned glasses and pours three fingers of single malt whiskey into each. He waits until the Special Agent finishes the file, walks back across the room, and hands him a glass. "Drink it. We'll have another before you leave this room. It will either be a toast to our continued association or to the parting of our ways."

John takes a long pull of the amber liquor before speaking. He slides the file across the table. "The FBI investigated me."

"And cleared you."

"What were the grounds for the investigation?"

"After Joy's death, you weren't acting within the normal range of grief, according to the shrinks. You didn't attend the funeral of your colleague, your lover, your child's mother. You haven't yet been to Joy's grave, or so I've been told."

John laughs—it's a laugh full of derision. "Given that Joy is still alive, Director, I'd say I made a prudent choice in staying away from her grave."

Gaffney pulls his whiskey.

John pushes back. "I took a leave of absence from FICA. That's how I dealt with Joy's death. You cleared my leave request, **Roland**," his word choice, intentional, but risky.

"John, you went AWOL after Joy's shooting. I didn't hear from you for three months. No calls, texts, emails, not even a message via carrier pigeon. You didn't log on to your systems, file a report, nothing—until you needed your FICA systems to figure out what Joy's final words meant. And, even then, you didn't sign back in to the Agency, you went rogue. I can be a patient man, John, but you tested my patience. Your actions, at best, were questionable, at worst, they were downright suspect. As a result, I was distracted by you at a time when I was up to my ass dealing with the unmasking of a valuable FICA asset, the preeminent cyber huntress, no less. I put eyes on you to prove that you **did not** unmask DOA. No matter your behavior, I never really believed that you had."

John takes another pull of whiskey and enjoys the burn before he addresses his boss. "You kept eyes on me for months. According to the investigative file, surveillance started immediately after Joy's death, and continued straight through the Montoya fiasco. You probably used the FBI detail assigned to Special Agent Shields to surveil me. How fortuitous— give her muscle when she's in town helping with the 'save Tess, save Annie' case, and since you're in Maxwell's neck of the woods, snoop on him, too. You sure like to kill two birds with one stone, Roland, I believe Roni's detail is the same detail who escorted me to this meeting, and is standing guard outside."

The Director nods. John pulls a sharp breath, and exhales sharp words. "You continued the surveillance when I was in New York working with the DEA on the Montoya and Hector cases. Explain."

Gaffney expects John's third and final sanctioned outburst at his next revelation. "You weren't the primary subject of the surveillance in New York. Veronica Shields was."

Are you in, or are you out?

There is no outburst from John. He silently finishes his whiskey, and sets his empty glass on the table. He leans back in his chair, stretches his legs, and lets his posture announce his disregard for that bit of news.

The Director drains his drink on his way back to the bar. He gets two more, carries them to the conference table. "John, now that you know Joy is alive, you need to find out who unmasked her. I should have had this talk with you before you went to Nice. I should have had you bring her back with you. She's at risk being out on her own. Granted, she is very good at being a ghost, but apparitions are seen from time to time. I believe you can attest to that." Gaffney gives a quick laugh and shake of his head before continuing. "Joy is the best, there's no disputing that. I've sent agents out looking for her, and they've either come back without getting eyes on her, or she gives them the slip. Still, my fear is that no matter how good Joy is, she will be found, taken hostage, or killed by enemy forces. I warned her before she left rehab, but she wanted out and since she was no longer an employee of FICA, I had no leverage over her. Technically, I shouldn't have sent field agents to Netti or helped her after the shooting.

When she crashed her system that morning, she was no longer a federal agent."

Heat is radiating off of John. The Director throws on some accelerant.

"When you started your thing with Roni Shields, you played into our hands. We loaned you to the DEA to finish the Montoya and Hector cases so you could get closer to Roni. Fortunately for us, you were completely on board with that part of the plan—without our manipulation."

John's slow burn picks up speed and heat.

"Part of your assignment, Special Agent Maxwell is to be with Special Agent Shields. In Seattle. In New York. In Mayflower. Wherever the hell you two want to be. Get close to her. She could be the one who unmasked Joy. You will have full access to FICA systems and any other agency you deem appropriate, so long as you investigate the unmasking of DOA. And if your investigation leads you away from Roni, well good for you two. When you are investigating her, Special Agent Maxwell, use your head and not the other part that you seem to favor with her. As for the other woman in your life, you will not communicate with Joy Ann Watts. If she contacts you, you are to inform me immediately. I am quite sure, however, that she won't make contact. We made a deal that she stays underground until we find out who unmasked her and the methods that were used. If she violates our agreement, I will put every agent in this building on her trail and bring her in."

"You allowed Joy to contact me in Nice?"

"Yes." There is finality in Gaffney's one word answer then a quick change in course. "John, you will have no other assignments until this situation is rectified. Until we know how and who unmasked DOA, this entire Agency and those who work with us are at risk."

"Have you ruled out Hector?"

"We have. Now it's your turn to rule him out or prove that he was responsible for Joy's unmasking. After you complete this assignment, you and I will be having a discussion as to what's next for you."

John sloshes what's been said through his semi-liquored-up brain, knowing he is about to be asked if he accepts or declines the assignment.

The FICA Director slides a whiskey toward the FICA Special Agent. "Are you in, or are you out?"

John stands from his seat. "I'll take the assignment, Director. As for the whiskey and this conversation, I've had enough."

"That's number three," the Director says as John walks out the door.

The Body

"The preeminent cyber defender, John Maxwell. He's not what I expected, given all that I've heard about the Boy Genius."

"You don't seem impressed," Gaffney pauses, "you should be. No one comes close to him in cyber defense, and no one is more motivated to get Joy Ann Watts back."

"You are wrong on that point, Roland. My motivation is preeminent. You'd be well served to remember that. What is your plan?"

"I gave Maxwell enough to work with. It won't be long before he realizes that my allegiances are no longer with FICA, and that I don't give a rat's ass about who did, or did not unmask DOA. That's when he'll realize that I want Joy Ann Watts, or more specifically, that I want DOA."

"Then…"

"His efforts to find his lifelong paramour will intensify. If anyone can find Joy Ann Watts, it's John Maxwell. When he does, he will lead us to her."

"And…"

"We take her, and eliminate him."

The Body walks to the door, and says over his shoulder, "If your plan fails, Roland, I will eliminate you."

Positively painful.

A black F150 is sitting on the driveway at Netti Farmhouse when the Feds pull up. Detective Fred Serpico exits his truck, Bob Seger's *Turn the Page* follows him out. He leans against the tailgate, puts one ankle over the other, and waits for John to approach him.

"Back from Nice a bit early, John."

The traveler nods. "Why are you here?"

"Just checking on the place. It's tight as a drum," Fred smiles, the wheels already turning in his head as to why John cut his month-long vacation short—by almost a month.

"Good to know." John tries to ignore the signs that the wheels are already turning in Fred's head. *Change the subject before the intrusive detective starts intruding and detecting.* John drops his travel bag and extends his hand. "I haven't formally congratulated you on the birth of your son."

Fred shakes John's hand nearly off his wrist and beams from ear to ear.

"You sure look happy, Fred. How's Kitt?"

"Happy and healthy. I like to think it's the boy, but it could be the sip or two of Moscato."

John smirks and nods.

"So, what's with the detail?" Fred sets one of his wheels in motion.

"Just a lift home from the airport."

"Pretty impressive lift. You get a promotion I don't know about?"

"It's no big deal. The crew cuts were at Logan—I was at Logan. They were the guys on Roni's detail during the 'save Tess, save Annie' case. They recognized me and gave me a lift."

"Good to know my taxpayer's money is going to good use," Fred scoffs.

John picks up his travel bag, a sign that the conversation is over. "Tell Kitt hello for me."

"Tell her yourself. Annie and Mike are coming to the bungalow for a barbecue later. They start law school soon and don't expect they'll have much free time after that. Stop by if you want. I'd like to show off my boy." Fred is still beaming from ear to ear as he drives away, the sound of Seger's *Against the Wind* blowing out the truck's windows.

John enters the farmhouse and places a call to Roni. It goes directly to voicemail.

"I'm home."

Bullet Bungalow
John can smell the barbecue from the driveway of the beachfront home of Kitt Mahoney. A fresh-faced beauty with long, wavy, nutty-brown hair and a million-watt smile, Kitt is every man's dream girl. She was John Maxwell's girl—until he turned the dream into a nightmare. The lucky man living the dream now is Detective Fred Serpico.

Welcoming cheers call out as John rounds the corner. As it so often happens, Kitt's get togethers tend to mushroom. Two becomes ten; ten becomes fifty, and so on. The Annie and Mike cookout now includes Fred's partner, Detective Steve Phelps and his significant other, Maura Putnam, who is Kitt's best friend, and a nurse practitioner at Mayflower-Falls Regional Medical Center. Manning the grill is David Cluster, a former Littleton College Police Sergeant, who recently became a cop with MFPD. With him is his Southern Belle, Jane Harper, who works at Littleton with Kitt, and is currently working the grill with her man. Officer Grant Speil is also amongst the barbecue guests and is holding hands with a hot Cougar Spinster with a mane of lion hair and dazzling sapphire blue eyes.

Holding center stage is a swaddled bundle named Joseph Mahoney Serpico. Currently, Master Joseph is happily settled in his father's arms, a place John suspects is familiar. Fred separates himself from the pack of oglers and brings his son to the arriving guest.

"Joseph, this is John Maxwell, aka Sam Sawyer." Fred leans close to his boy and whispers in his ear, "I'll tell you all about him when you're older. John, meet Joseph." Fred's smile is beyond wide and looks positively painful.

"Hey, little guy." Johns takes a long stare at the boy, then runs a bent-at-the-knuckle finger gently down the boy's cheek. "He's a looker, Fred. Congratulations, again."

The men are interrupted by Kitt—the quintessential earth mother. The Evangeline Lilly lookalike has her hair pulled high, is wearing a gauzy dress of white, and a smile from ear to ear. She steps into John's open arms. "I'm glad you came."

Given the myriad of secrets and lies that were revealed about John shortly before Joy's death, the man finds it remarkable that he is welcome at the bungalow. He fully recognizes that his acceptance back into the fold is a testament to the woman who recently brought this baby boy into the world, the one whose temple he kisses.

"Kitt, he's a great looking boy. You sure he's Fred's?"

Fred laughs big.

John walks with Kitt to the porch, "Have you heard from Callie and Tess?" the father asks with a measure of guilt for not having seen them in months or talked to them in weeks.

"They called yesterday. The basketball and swim camp at Assumption College in Worcester is everything they hoped it would be. Tess says Callie is the star of the basketball camp. Apparently, she has untapped skills that the college coaches recognized, and after working with her, I guess she's tearing up the court."

"And Tess?"

"She's caught the eye of a swim coach. Callie says Tess is a natural. She takes the turns with power and paces herself, leaving enough energy to grab the win. But she's also making her moves on the court along with Callie."

John motions his head toward the Atlantic. "Her swimming strength probably comes from the ocean workouts. The waves made her strong."

"That's exactly what Callie said," Kitt nudges. She raises a hand to block the lowering sun from her eyes, and looks at her high school sweetheart, the father of her three girls, the man who hurt her deeply and who is working hard to make amends. "You look..."

"Tired," he interrupts. "It's jet lag."

"Good, because I was thinking you look troubled." Kitt takes his hand. "Come on, John, let's get you fed."

The tired and troubled man arrives back at Netti Farmhouse around 8 PM, goes directly to his room, and crashes. He doesn't bother looking for a message from Roni. He knows there won't be one, and he knows he doesn't care.

Go to Nice, she says.

Private investigator, Bill Bettke, places a call to his boss. She doesn't answer the call. She hasn't answered any of his calls for a week. Bettke wants to update the woman who sent him across the Atlantic giving him nothing more than a picture of a stunning blonde woman and an NFL QB lookalike. He wants to brag about his PI skills—he did, after all, find two American needles in a European haystack. He wants to tell her that no matter how brief their meeting, contact between the two was made. Bettke doesn't know who the waif woman or the buff dude are, but he knows he is near to losing an opportunity. He intersected with the mystery woman days after she gave him and everyone else the slip. He wants to follow her out of Nice, but he isn't doing it on his dime. "If I don't follow her now, I may not pick up the trail again! That's why you need to answer the damn phone!" he yells before slipping it into his pocket.

Bettke needs a drink. He mutters as he moves along the now familiar cobblestones of Nice looking for a bar. "'Go to Nice,' she says. 'I want you to find this woman,' she says. 'See if she meets this man,' she says. 'If you find them, trail them until one of them leaves Nice.' I find the woman. I find the man. He leaves Nice. She's leaving Nice. Boss Lady you have 24-hours to say something else, or I'm flying back to the

States." He pulls open a pastel yellow door of a tiny bar, Bibine, and steps inside for a few bières.

Seattle

Roni pulls herself away from her office window after a full day of processing. She angrily grabs her briefcase, purse, cell phone, and jacket, and heads for the door. She is just about through it when her cell rings. She checks caller ID: **Bill Bettke**. She ignores the call. It's the fifth she's received from him that day. "I'm not ready to know the answer," she says before sending the call directly to voicemail.

Sainte Marguerite

Joy wakes a bit later than usual on the largest of four islands off the coast of Cannes. She boarded a ferry from Quai Lunel, the day before, for a 2-hour cruise from Nice to Saint Tropez, but cut her waterway trip short after hearing fellow passengers rave about Sainte Marguerite's lush nature along Bateguier Pond. She hasn't yet ventured to the water, or communed with the flora and fauna, as is her preferred way of things. She spent most of the previous day making sure no one followed her from the mainland, then hiked in and set camp.

The sun is already bright and rising fast in a brilliant azure sky as Joy lifts her head off her duffle. Though still cool in the thick, she can tell her day's trek is going to be a hot one. She stretches and smiles, knowing she is prepared for whatever the day brings. Whenever she takes up temporary residence, she stocks up on provisions for the emergency backpacking excursions that are part of her life now. "Always be prepared. Do whatever it takes to survive." She repeats the FBI training charge, then scoffs. "Stay away from the fucking FBI is what I need to do to survive." She laughs big, notices that it sounds a bit unhinged, which makes her laugh even harder, "Irony isn't dead—and neither am I." Her prolonged chuckles cut the tranquility around her.

She grabs hold of her wits, and a package of baby wipes from the duffle and freshens up while she munches on some granola and sips some water. She pulls the curly brunette wig she's worn for two days from her head, tucks it into the duffle, and pours a good amount of water onto her hair. "Well, *that* sure kept the insects out—although it's itchy and hot as fuck." She lets the cool water run down her face and neck while she rummages for a bandana that she wets and ties around her forehead. Before packing up her gear, she reviews her new ID packet, and checks the cash that she rolled and tucked inside a hollowed-out soda can. "Okay. You're prepared. You can relax, now." The Special Agent can't relax, but she can breathe, at least for a little bit.

Before setting out on her trek, Joy opens the newspaper she bought when she arrived on the island and reads the weather forecast for the next couple days. "Sunny and hot. So far, it's A+ on today's forecast." She reads the long-range predictions and makes a plan. "If the meteorologists are consistently accurate, then I'll need to find shelter if I'm still on the island three days from now." Finished with her morning attending, Joy delights in the stillness of the woods. Nature's cacophony keeps her company—calling, whistling, and shrieking birds, chirping crickets, an occasional slither here and snapping branch there—they all remind her that she is connected to *something*. After a minute of bliss, the former Special Agent cautions herself as to why she is on an island in the Mediterranean. "The Body wants you." She touches the gun strapped to one ankle and the knife sheathed to the other.

It's a little early, but.

John has been at the barn for hours, though he has done nothing more than logon to his systems. That's because Gaffney's words have been banging the shit out of his head all night long.

"I want you unarmed, Special Agent Maxwell. I believe you might shoot me when I tell you a story. — You should address me as Director for this meeting, Special Agent Maxwell. — I'm going to give you an assignment. If you refuse the assignment, you will be released from FICA. — Now that you know Joy is alive, you need to find out who unmasked her. — You will have no other assignments until this situation is rectified. — After you complete this assignment, you and I will be having a discussion as to what's next for you. — Are you in, or are you out?"

After the hundredth or so loop he decides, "The Director never said I can't get help with the investigation." John checks the clock, "It's a little early, but..."

Bullet Bungalow
Fred nestles Joseph next to an exhausted Kitt. She rests her head on her outstretched arm and

inches her baby toward her breast. Joseph latches on and goes to work.

"Kittridge, I'm happy."

"I am too, Fred, blissfully so," she practically purrs.

A lovely silence embraces the new family. Sadly, silence is too easily broken. Fred's cell phone vibrates on the end table. He picks it up and checks the caller ID. "It's John."

"Something's up with him. He said it was jet lag, but it's not," Kitt says.

"We'll see," Fred pushes the answer button. "It's early, John."

"Too early for a trip to Netti?"

"Nope."

"I'm in the barn."

Fred gives his baby boy and his woman a kiss on their heads, and drags his ass out of bed. "I'm heading to Netti. Something's up with John." From halfway across the room, he calls over his shoulder, "And you can stop smirking, Kittridge. That's John and Annie's thing."

Netti

It only takes one look at John Maxwell, for Fred Serpico to know that something big is up. The detective isn't even all the way in to the barn and he's detecting a shitload of tension and heat radiating off of the Special Agent—the one who usually has no "tell".

"You look like…"

"—I haven't slept?"

"I was gonna say that you look like shit." Fred moves to where John is, making sure he leaves a wide span between them. He leans against a counter and crosses one ankle over the other, then immediately uncrosses it just in case. "Actually, you look like you want to take the head off someone."

"Several someones."

"Present company excluded, right?"

"Right."

Fred waits for John to start. The wait isn't long.

"What's the most shocking thing that's ever happened to you?"

Fred eyes the crazy man.

John gets up from his seat and steps into Fred's buffer zone. "Answer the question."

"The most shocking thing? I don't know, John. Are you gonna shock me by saying you and Roni are hitched?"

John laughs big. John never laughs big. "Take a seat, Fred."

"I'd rather stay standing. I'm getting the feeling that I might need to make a hasty retreat."

"Suit yourself. Joy is alive."

Fred pauses, only in that way a person who has been shot pauses before they fall to the ground. He slowly pushes his ass off the counter, takes a few steps, and drops his ass onto a chair with a thud. Minutes pass before Fred pulls himself to a standing position. He walks past John, "Follow me," he climbs to the second floor loft, and points to a set of stairs across from the ones they just ascended. "Correct me if I'm wrong on this point, ten months ago I saw you climb those stairs right there as I climbed these. I saw Hector standing at that window seconds after he shot Joy Ann Watts. I saw you shoot the fucker. I watched you pull your terrified daughter off of the floor and into your arms, and then look out that window at a felled Joy Ann Watts. I stood vigil for Joy at Mayflower-Falls Regional. I felt the wind leave me when they pronounced her dead. I helped Kittridge plan Joy's funeral. I attended Joy's funeral. I **paid** for Joy's funeral. And now, you're telling me that Joy Ann Watts is alive."

John nods, but says nothing.

Fred turns and heads back down the stairs calling over his shoulder, "I don't know what the hell is going on, but I do know one thing. I want my money back."

This is some serious shit.

The men head to the farmhouse and take seats at the kitchen table. John jumps right in. "I was sitting at an outdoor café in Nice wondering what the hell I was doing in France. I was just about to leave when I felt a touch on my shoulder and heard a woman say, 'I knew you'd come'. I turned toward the voice and saw Joy standing within arm's reach. The woman who is supposedly dead and buried in Mayflower-Falls Cemetery approached me on a cobblestone alleyway in Old Town. I managed to ask two questions, How? and Why? She answered neither; she simply said, 'I'm being watched. I can't stay'. I stood there, like a damned statue, and watched a 'dead' woman walk away. When I got my mental shit together, I started looking for her. I spent the remainder of that day wandering aimlessly around the seaside village searching for a ghost. When I returned to my hotel room that night, I found this slipped under my door." He hands Fred the note.

Fred reads it out loud. "Find out who unmasked me – find out who is after me." He starts to say something.

John shakes his head, and continues. "I spent the next few days **not** searching for Joy. I knew I wasn't going to find her, and more to the point, I didn't want to lead the tall, black, hippy dude to her."

"Tail?"

"Yeup. After leading him astray for a couple days, I called it quits and headed stateside. My plan was to come here and regroup, then go to FICA to find out what the hell is going on. FICA came to me, instead. When I arrived at Logan, I was escorted from the plane to a 'leave your weapons outside the door' meeting with Director Gaffney. He said he wanted me unarmed while he told me a story, afterwards he was going to give me an assignment, and if I refused it I would be released from service."

"I hope you refused it. FICA is a cesspool," Fred quips.

"Wait until you hear how deep a cesspool."

Fred nods. "Continue."

"First, Gaffney said he knew I saw Joy in Nice. Then he started explaining what transpired over the past ten months. The morning of the shooting Joy crashed her FICA systems because she was unmasked. He told her he would send a team of agents to Netti to bring her in for her protection. Part of the team he sent was a medically trained FICA unit. They didn't bring Joy to Mayflower-Falls Regional after she was shot. They worked on her in the ambulance, during a med-flight, and at a secure medical facility."

Fred starts to say something, stops when he sees the shake of John's head.

"After that dog and pony show, he turned his attention to me. He handed me a file—an investigative and surveillance file conducted on yours truly. During the time when I thought I was on authorized bereavement leave, Gaffney considered me AWOL."

Fred interrupts this time. "Damn, John, this is some serious shit."

"It gets worse. After the initial investigation was concluded, he kept me under surveillance, or so I thought based on the file I'd read. Gaffney confirmed that when I was in New York working with the DEA on the Montoya and Hector cases, FICA was watching—turns out the primary subject of that surveillance was Roni."

Fred shifts in his seat. He has something to say, but he lets John finish.

"This is when Gaffney went all Don Corleone on me, making the offer that I can't refuse. He told me that I have to find out who unmasked Joy. He said he should have told me she was alive before I went to Nice, so I could have brought her in. He said he warned her before she left rehab that she'd be in danger on her own, but he had to let her go since she no longer worked for FICA. Then he pivoted back to Roni. Gaffney wants me *with* Roni, to do an 'up close and personal' investigation on her, to find out if she unmasked Joy. I'll have access to any federal agency I need, so long as I work on this and only this investigation—regardless of where it leads. I guess that means I have the help of the DEA, which means that Special Agent, Veronica Shields, is now on the radar of my boss and maybe her boss."

"Shit, John."

"There's more."

"Shit, John."

"Gaffney said I am not allowed to communicate with Joy, and if she contacts me, I need to notify him. He's confident that she won't initiate contact because they have an agreement—she remains underground until the person who unmasked her is identified. If she violates their agreement, he will use every agent he has to find her and bring her in. I asked Gaffney if he allowed Joy to contact me in Nice. He had a one word answer: 'Yes'. I asked him if he ruled out Hector as the person who unmasked DOA. He said FICA had, but it's my turn to rule him in or out. The last thing he said was, 'After completion of this assignment, you and I will be having a discussion as to what's next for you'."

After a pause, Fred asks, "You done?"

"Yeup."

Fred gets up from the table and goes to the living room bay window. After several minutes of processing he calls over his shoulder, "Well, that explains your taxpayer-funded lift home from Logan." He spends a few more minutes looking outside then heads back to the kitchen. "So that's it?"

John smirks. "That's not enough? I don't think I've said that many consecutive words in my entire life."

"Oh, it's enough. But straight up, I have a question. Since you and Roni weren't the only people who knew Joy Ann Watts was DOA, why are you two the focus? Why did Gaffney lean into her former lover and her former friend?" Fred heads to the back porch and looks out over John's farmland for a few. While he processes, John gets up and puts on a pot of coffee, then hops up onto the counter.

"Okay, if Director Gaffney wants you to investigate, then let's investigate – **everyone** – who knew the identity of DOA. So, who knew?"

"Off the top, Gaffney knew; he was the one who put Joy Dead On Assignment fifteen years ago. His second-in-command, Stacy Remington, knew, and the Director of the FBI, Shelby Webber, knew. When Annie infiltrated my systems and compromised DOA, Gaffney brought in five agents to help with Hector's ramped-up attacks and investigate how DOA was compromised. Those five agents were probably told some, maybe all, of Joy's background."

Fred tallies. "So, we've got you, Roni, Gaffney, Remington, Webber, and five FICA agents who knew Joy was DOA. Then, we've got Hector who might have known. He unmasked you right before the shooting, so there's nothing to say he didn't unmask DOA, too. How about the CIA, DEA, Homeland Security, anyone at those agencies, or their counterparts in the U.K. who might have known?"

"If anyone at the agencies were told outright, it would have been the higher-ups, but those bureaus do their own investigative and intelligence gathering, so it's possible field agents found out the identity of the Dead On Assignment agent. There are three people at British Intelligence who know that the preeminent cyber huntress is a U.S. agent. While they've known about her for years, it's against Agency protocol that they were told her true identity. It's highly unlikely that they unmasked her because she's as valuable an asset to them, as she is to us. Generally speaking, it would be tough going for anyone to unmask her. Joy was a ghost in cyberland, and she didn't exist on paper in the real world. The closest anyone got was Hector when he connected the cyber huntress to her Agency name, Fee Peterson."

"So far as we know."

John nods.

Fred nods. "We won't consider the agencies, foreign or domestic, as suspect pools unless our investigation leads us to them. So, we're still at eleven initial investigations."

John corrects Fred. "Ten. Roni, Gaffney, Webber, Remington, five FICA agents, and Hector."

Fred corrects John. "Eleven. You're not ruled out until we rule you out. You're a suspect, too, Special Agent Maxwell."

Batting 0 for 2.

Roni can't sleep. That's because she listened to the PI's messages. Twice. Which torqued her up. Twice. She checks her bedside clock for the umpteenth time, 4:44 AM. She angrily pushes away her covers, drags herself from bed, and slides open her patio doors. She rubs her hands vigorously along the gooseflesh that covers her arms, and looks out at the darkened skyline of Seattle. Scattered flecks of light in distant buildings lets her know she isn't the only tortured soul awake. "That's little comfort," she admits. She takes a deep cleansing breath, exhaling with it any hope that she will find rest that night. "Make the call. You sent him to find out. He found out. Now make the damned call." She walks back inside, and makes the damned call, "Follow her." She crawls back into bed, and waits for her alarm to ring—it's a fifteen minute wait.

Nice
Bettke settles his bill with the bartender for his lunch and a few bières, apparently a few too many bières. He stumbles out into the bright sunshine and bangs along the cobblestone streets to the last place he saw her, Quai Lunel. He practically bumped into her after days of searching, then followed her to Old Port. He watched her buy a one-way ticket to Saint

Tropez then take a seat on a bench to soak up the sun, and wait for her water lift. She wore a curly brunette wig and big plastic sunglasses, but he knew it was his mark. "It's her smile. She can't alter that." He wipes sweat from his brow, and pushes deep for clarity. "Was she here *yesterday*?" He tries to clear his liquored-up brain with a vigorous shake of his head. "Yes. Yes. She was here, yesterday."

By the time he's hoofed it back to the dock, he is more clear-headed, and sure-footed. The PI shows the waif woman's photo to several dock workers. Two confirm that that they saw her board a ferry to Saint Tropez the day before, then comment that the beautiful woman looks like Amanda Seyfried. Bettke shrugs at the reference, then boards the next water taxi to the next beautiful coastal town on his mystery tour of the Mediterranean. When he arrives at the bustling Port de Saint Tropez, he shows his mark's picture to a group of dock workers. He receives headshakes on her arrival, **and** unanimity that she looks like Amanda Seyfried. One worker suggests, "If she's on Saint Tropez, she will head to the fishing village of La Ponche or to the beach of Pampelonne." After an afternoon of searching and waiting, Bettke accepts that he is batting 0 for 2 on finding the waif woman. He walked and talked his way through the two tourist locations, and while no one confirmed seeing her, they all agreed that she looks like Amanda Seyfried. As he walks back to the dock, he wonders aloud, "Who the hell is Amanda Seyfried?"

Sainte Marguerite

Joy spends an itchy night and morning in the heavily wooded area she set as her campsite the first day she arrived on the island. The itch she's experiencing has nothing to do with the outdoors. This itch tells her that someone is tight on her tail.

Saint Tropez

Bill Bettke spends the rest of the afternoon roaming the internationally acclaimed seaside resort. With each step he takes, at each stop he makes, his gut tells him she isn't there. The seasoned PI should be listening to his gut, it is almost always right—just like it was back in Nice. The seasoned pro from Washington State knew he wasn't the only one with eyes on the waif woman. He honed in on a black hippie with long dreads who'd already had her in his sights. Bettke hadn't a clue why Dreadhead was on her trail, but then again, he hasn't a clue why he's in the south of France, either. As the PI searches for his mark, he keeps an eye out for Dreadhead. He comes up empty on both fronts. "Where the fuck are they? I wasted too much time waiting for the go-ahead from Seattle. Now that I've got it, I need to start from scratch."

The overheated PI heads to a local travel agency, welcomes the tiny blast of cool air when he enters, makes his way to a display rack, and does a little memory recall.

"Your subject likes quaint villages and outdoor venues. You won't find her at a museum or gallery, so don't bother with those. Think birds, trees, and ponds, then go there."

His boss gave him that tip shortly before he boarded the 12-hour flight from Seattle to Paris. "Not much to go on," he grouses, but... He eyes the countless brochures on the twirling rack while he connects some dots. "If she left Nice on a ferry headed to Saint Tropez and never got there, then she got off..." He ponders the Mediterranean coastline, "She could have gotten off in Cannes...but why spend the extra bucks on a ticket from Nice to Saint Tropez? Unless, getting off was an impulse, or... the trip to Saint Tropez was a ruse." He ponders. He decides. "The ferry from Nice to Saint Tropez stops at these small islands." He pulls four brochures—four very specific brochures. "This group of islands are between Nice and Saint Tropez, and just off the coast of Cannes" He gives them a quick look—puts three back almost immediately. He considers the one for Sainte Marguerite as particularly interesting. "Nature, culture, botanical trails. A pond with a bunch of birds," he reads out loud. *Bingo!*

Bettke boards the last ferry of the day from Saint Tropez to Sainte Marguerite.

Joy boards the last ferry of the day from Sainte Marguerite to Cannes.

Yeah, well I should have.

Kitt puts her contented baby into his crib. It is front and center in the beige and navy adorned nursery that was once the mini master of his oldest sister, Annie. Momma places a finger-kiss to her boy's head then races through the bungalow, hoping to catch Fred before he sneaks out. She is lying in wait on the back porch when he tries to do just that. "Going somewhere?" she asks.

Fred laughs at the porch creeper. "Kittridge, I can't. The moment I can, I promise you I will." He bends and kisses his woman, then yells back to her as he rounds the corner of the bungalow, "Kittridge, I'm happy."

Kittridge Anne Mahoney nestles onto the porch sofa and takes in the sights and sounds of *her* ocean, feeling very happy herself.

MFPD
Fred travels the main streets of Mayflower sans the customary sounds of Mr. Bob Seger filling his F-150. When he enters the MFPD station, he finds Detective Steve Phelps doing something Detective Steve Phelps almost never does— he's relaxing. He has his feet up on his desk, arms crossed behind his head, and is leaning so far back in his chair that Fred wonders how he

stays upright. "Wish Sir Isaac Newton could see you defying gravity over there."

"Hey, Fred, didn't see you yesterday. Everything alright at home?"

"Kittridge says, 'everything is blissful'."

"Well, Kitt is never wrong, my friend."

"You have **no** idea how right you are, partner."

"How so?"

"When Kittridge saw John at the barbecue the other night, she said there was something up with him. She was right. And it's *big*. Steve, it's real *big*."

The detective kicks his feet off his desk. "Guess that's all the relaxing I'm gonna get."

"For a l.o.n.g. t.i.m.e. my friend."

"What's going on?"

Fred shakes his head and takes a seat—Fred rarely takes a seat. "John is in a jam at work. He's being forced to investigate a certain matter and depending on the outcome of the investigation he may or may not be a Secret Agent Man when he's done. He asked for my help and said I could bring you along for the ride, if you want in, that is."

"Why wouldn't I want in? We've all moved on from the blowback of John's lies about being a super-spy. If we handled that mess, why not this?"

"Detective Phelps, you don't know the particulars of this investigation. This situation is **big**. Emphasis on the word, **fucking**."

"You didn't say the word, fucking," Steve laughs.

"Yeah? Well, I should have. This situation is fucking big! John and I have no idea what we will uncover, but we do know this, when the shit hits the fan, we are going to be breathing the stench. You need to know that before you tread in."

Steve gets up from his desk and begins pacing.

Fred gets up from his desk and takes his usual spot at the window. He looks out over the sleepy streets of Mayflower wondering if the men will be able to keep Joy alive this time around—once they find her, that is.

Steve joins Fred at the window. "I'm in."

Detective Fred Serpico and Detective Steve Phelps arrive at Netti Farmhouse shortly before 10 AM. The back door is wide open.

"No need for the B&E." Steve slaps Fred across the shoulder.

"Maxwell is no fun."

John calls out, "Back here."

The men make their way to John's version of a family room. Fred named the windowless room "the cave" and would refuse to head that way had the room not saved the lives of every woman he holds near and dear during the whole 'save Tess, save Annie' nightmare. The space is designed specifically for a Secret Agent Man. It is wood paneled with built-in bookcases, secret latches, and sliding sections. Tucked behind the paneling is a hidden safe place and a storage area for an ammunitions and weapons cache. Rich oxblood leather furniture and an impressive fieldstone fireplace fill the rest of the space. Fred enters the dreaded cave and stretches out on the couch. Steve takes the empty chair near the fireplace.

"John, fill Steve in on everything you told me yesterday. Leave nothing out. I'm gonna close my eyes for a minute." Fred listens to John's opening words...

"I arrived in Nice on August 1. On August 4, I was sitting at an outdoor café. I felt a touch on my shoulder and heard a woman say, 'I knew you'd come...'"

Fred drifts off with two of John's words banging in his head, **How? and Why?**

John calls to Fred from across the room, "Hey, Sleeping Beauty, how do I turn him off?"

The exhausted father of a newborn cracks open one eye, then the other. "How long has he been pacing?"

"Since you fell asleep an hour ago."

"Give him five minutes, then I'll turn him off."

John leaves the cave muttering, "You guys are freaks." When he returns, he's still spewing. "Last time I was this dizzy, I was on some torturous spinning teacup with a three year old."

"Hey, partner. You about done with the pacing?"

The huffing and puffing man takes one final lap, then lands his ass on the chair near the fireplace.

Fred claps his hands once and starts. "I was up most of the night thinking about the best way to attack this investigation. Questions, one right after the other, started banging in my head. All of them were vying for 'top dog'. It wasn't until I heard John start repeating the *Joy is Alive – So What's New With You* story that I had a thought. We're going to concentrate on the questions John asked Joy: How? and Why? First up, how did Joy become unmasked? In general terms, what does it take to unmask a covert spy? Hector tried to unmask Sam Sawyer for more than a decade. He couldn't do it without the help of a teenager. Up until the time that Annie compromised DOA, Hector had nothing, and he was supposed to be one of the best cyber hunters in the world. His inability suggests that unmasking someone is hard work."

"It's supposed to be," John states the obvious.

"But it can be done, case in point, Hector unmasked you," Fred pushes.

"With a lot of help," John defends. "My cyber walls are impenetrable. That's why I was Hector's nemesis. As good as he was supposed to be, he wasn't good enough to get me. That's why he hunted Joy. When he got the thread to pull on DOA, and figured there was a connection between the preeminent huntress and the preeminent hunter, he honed in on her. DOA was a much easier target. While I was building walls to avoid detection, Joy was diving deep. The shallow swimmers in cyberland never knew about her, but the deep divers knew there was a preeminent huntress. Some knew, others assumed that she worked for the U.S., and many others thought she was a free agent. Allies made sure they didn't do anything that would inadvertently unmask her. Adversaries of the United States had cyber teams solely dedicated *to* unmasking her—*everyone* wanted the preeminent huntress on their team, or dead."

Fred grunts, "So, why did Gaffney put all his chips on you?"

"What?"

"When Hector honed in on DOA and tried to unmask her, why didn't the Director of FICA take his best defender—the one who built the best cyber walls in the world—off of everything else, and have you defend the 'preeminent cyber huntress'? Why did he protect you, and leave her vulnerable?"

John is quiet for a few before opining, "Gaffney's main focus with FICA was always defense. The terrorist attacks on U.S. soil inflamed him, and set his professional agenda. He never tried to hide his bias about defense versus offense."

"Yeah, but without Joy's work in cyberland, without her getting intel about potential attacks, the defensive team wouldn't know who was coming and what they had in the works," Steve casually tosses in his two cents.

"John, keep talking. Just free-flow it," Fred directs.

"Cyber hunters live in the deep. Their work necessitates that they be in perpetual motion, ergo, they are perpetually vulnerable. DOA was a huntress, the best huntress. She didn't build walls, she ghosted through them. Bottom line, the possibilities of who might have unmasked her are virtually endless. This investigation is going to be like looking for a needle in cyberspace."

That makes no sense.

Steve jumps in. "I'm hung up on a why question. It's been bothering me since the shooting. Why did Hector kill Joy and not John? The maniac who wanted to be the Boy Genius of cyberland spent more than a decade trying to find out who the covert agent, Sam Sawyer was. The reason he wanted to know who his nemesis was, is because he wanted to kill him.

When Hector finally learned that John Maxwell was the man behind the persona, Sam Sawyer, what did he do? He took John's daughter to John's place of business, to lure John to a death match. **That makes sense**. And when John Maxwell showed up for his date with destiny what did Hector do? He let his nemesis, his proclaimed Achilles, walk away without so much as a skirmish. **That does not make sense**. Answer this if you can. Why didn't Hector focus all of his efforts on killing John, especially when it became obvious that the maniac wasn't going to make it out of Netti Barn alive. Furthermore, Kitt said that DOA took a bullet meant for her. That begs this question. Who the hell was Hector really after that morning? It sure as hell wasn't John Maxwell."

Fred smiles wide at John. "That's why I put up with the damn pacing, Special Agent Maxwell."

John smirks.

Fred pushes in. "Steve, that's a dig deep question. Hopefully, we'll get a thread to pull when we move through the others, like how did FICA Director, Roland Gaffney, get agents to Netti Barn as quickly as he did? The whole incident that morning, from the time John and I left Bullet Bungalow to the shooting of Hector at Netti Barn, couldn't have been more than two hours, tops. The closest FBI field office from Mayflower is an hour away in Boston. Gaffney told John that after Joy's call to him that morning he arranged for agents to go to Netti. Let's look at the logistics of that. The Director would need time to assign agents and get them up to speed. And according to him, the agents were medically trained, so there's that piece, which means more time. Then he needed to outfit the agents as EMTs, procure an ambulance, get them into the ambulance, and get that ambulance to Netti Barn. All of that cannot be done in two hours. It feels like this plan was already in motion. So, the question of how he managed to do all of that is interesting, but the question of why he did it is significant. Why did Director Gaffney want to get Joy into protective custody after she was unmasked? Who did he think was after her?"

"Everyone was after her," John reminds Fred.

"Okay, but why did Gaffney go to extreme measures for Joy **after** she crashed her systems? Why did he send a medical team to Netti? Why didn't that team take her to the nearest hospital? Why did his team take her to an airstrip? Why was there a med-flight waiting at that airstrip? Why did Gaffney's team take her to a secure medical facility?"

"…where he was waiting for her to arrive," John adds.

"Right. And why is Gaffney sending agents to try to find her if she's supposedly underground? It's counterintuitive. Furthermore, Gaffney didn't provide DOA protection during the whole Hector thing, so why is he going to great lengths to keep her alive and in his sights when she doesn't even work for him?"

John's answer is immediate. "Maybe Gaffney figured out that Annie was the one who compromised DOA, and that I covered it up. Maybe he's providing protection for Joy now because he didn't give it to her then, and maybe he's meting out punishment to me at the same time. Gaffney said he investigated me because I went AWOL. What if he investigated me because I didn't admit it was Annie who compromised DOA. That lie calls into question everything I have or haven't done as an agent of FICA. It's also a reminder to the Director that he protected me, and in doing so, his best cyber huntress was unmasked, and 'killed'. If Gaffney knows all this, and he holds me responsible for all this, then he's pissed."

Steve scoffs, "That's a lot of maybes, John, but I'll play along. Maybe Gaffney's up to no good."

"No maybes about it," Fred tosses in, "but let's pull the threads before concluding."

Fred starts a new set of how and why questions. "How did Roni get the attention of the FICA Director?"

Steve jumps in on this. "Because Roni and Joy broke interagency protocol and continued a secret friendship. The linchpin of DOA's work was that she didn't exist. DOA was a ghost, not the dead variety that she supposedly is now, but the super-spy variety. Joy gave up everything when she went Dead On Assignment, at least that's what she was supposed to have done. Gaffney sanctioned the ABC Love Tours between the super-spies, but the covert Special Agent wasn't supposed to maintain a relationship with anyone else. I don't think Gaffney would take kindly to Joy's disobedience. There was too much on the line— for the nation and for the Director. Furthermore, DOA was Gaffney's brainchild. I'm sure he harbors proprietary notions about Joy. Can't imagine he wants to share her with anyone. I think we should figure out if Gaffney knew about the women's forbidden relationship and if so, when he found out about it."

John interjects, "Gaffney is a stickler for protocol. If he knew about them, he would have gone the disciplinary route."

Steve counters, "Unless Gaffney benefitted somehow by letting them continue a friendship. Case in point, if you're right, and he knows you covered up Annie's involvement in outing DOA, and he didn't fire you outright, it's because he benefits somehow. Guys like Gaffney play their hands, John, that's how he forced you into handling this investigation." Steve looks over at Fred. "You're working a different angle over there."

"Yeah. Something's gnawing at me, but I can't get at it." He leaves the cave and stands at the living room bay window hoping he can grab hold of whatever thread is twisting in the wind.

Seattle
Roni is in her home office staring at the piece of paper she placed on her desk nearly an hour before. There are only three words on that piece of paper.

Joy is alive.

Roni picks up her pen and forces herself to work the problems associated with those three words.

Joy is alive.

1. Did John know that Joy was alive?
2. Is that why he wanted to continue the alphabetical reunions?
3. If John knew, why did he get involved with me?
4. If John knew, why did he invite me to go to Nice?
5. Did John give me an either-or choice so I'd end our relationship?
6. Is that how he kept me from going to Nice?
7. What's John's next move?
8. What's my next move?

Who's in that casket?

Kitt is communing with her ocean when Fred arrives home. He smiles wide as he approaches. "Kittridge, how much wine can you drink while you're breastfeeding?"

"About four-ounces a day, why?"

"Because when I tell you what's going on, you're gonna want a whole bottle—correction, you're gonna need a whole bottle."

"Then it's a good thing I've got plenty of breastmilk in the freezer."

"Wait here. I'll go grab a bottle – of **your** yumminess – not the boy's yumminess," he laughs. The devilishly dimpled detective returns with a wine glass and a bottle of Kitt's favorite Moscato in hand. The eagerly awaiting woman has taken a perch on the porch sofa, her legs tucked tight beneath her—as is her preferred way of things.

Fred chuckles. "Good. You're sitting—sort of."

"Fred Serpico, your news better be big after all this fanfare." She sends one of her million-watt dazzlers at her man.

He proceeds to get lost in the beauty of Kittridge Anne Mahoney. Her usual athletic form is soft and full in all the right places from her pregnancy with Joseph. She is the quintessential earth momma right now, sexy in a way that's different than before. He aches...

Kitt clears her throat, "Fred, I'm dying over here."

"Ditto!" he snaps, then catches the tilt of her head and raising of her brow. He pulls himself back to the reason they're on the porch. "Right, you're dying for the story."

"For the wine," she corrects and laughs.

He pours a glass and hands it to the wanting woman. "First, the rules. Not one word of what I tell you leaves this porch. Not. One. Word. You do not speak of this to anyone but me. No one. Do you accept the rules, Kittridge?"

"Yes."

"Look at my face so you will know I'm not kidding around when I tell you."

Kitt is rapt with attention.

"Joy is alive."

Kitt is too stunned to drink her Moscato. She **needs** her Moscato, but she is incapable of bringing the glass to her lips, of taking a sip, and swallowing her effervescent yumminess.

Fred is pulled from the moment by the squawking that's coming from the nursery. He leaves a dumbfounded Kitt sitting on the back porch, puts a bag of frozen breast milk into a bowl of warm water to defrost, then sprints to the nursery to tend to his boy. "Well hello, Joseph. There's no need for all the noise. Come on, little guy, let's get you changed and fed. If you're a good boy, I'll take you out onto the porch to see your momma. Daddy accidently turned her into a statue. It was quite a thing to see." Fred buzzes his contented son's cheek, bundles him in a blanket, and brings him out to Kitt. He whispers into Joseph's ear, "See, Momma hasn't moved a muscle since Daddy left her." Fred sits next to Kitt, crosses one leg over the other, puts his son onto the crook of his knee, and the bottle's nipple into his mouth. He nudges Kitt with his shoulder. "You still breathing?"

His woman's beautiful acorn-brown eyes still hold the shock of hearing the words, "Joy is alive." She is staring out at the waning sunlight that's sparkling on gentle waves that hold her in their hypnotic embrace. She speaks in hushed tones, as though not wanting to disturb the moment. "When you say Joy is alive, you are referring to Joy Ann Watts, right?"

Fred nods.

"Answer in words, Fred."

"Yes, Joy Ann Watts is alive."

"Fred, you'd tell me if I was having some sort of postpartum break from reality, right?"

"Yes."

"Or if I concussed my head and don't remember the events at Netti Barn?"

"Yes."

"Or if we are actors in a soap opera like *Dallas* and instead of Bobby Ewing being in the shower, Kitt is on the porch realizing the past year is a dream?"

"Yes."

"Or if we are in some other soap opera where people come back from the dead? Oh, Fred, when they come back, they usually look like someone else. Does Joy look like Joy? Oh, I hope so, she's so pretty. Don't you think so, Fred? Joy is so pretty."

The dimpled detective laughs. "It's none of those things." He nudges her wine glass toward her lips. "I really think you need some of this. Drink."

Time surrenders many minutes while Kitt tries to process Chapter 1 of the *Joy Is Alive – So What's New With You* story. Her efforts are impeded by a severely stunned brain. Sounds of waves meeting the shoreline have lulled Joseph to sleep, and have pulled his momma into some sort of trance. She hasn't asked another question, sipped any of her yumminess, or blinked an acorn.

Fred puts Joseph onto his shoulder, stands up, and extends his hand to his woman, who does absolutely nothing. Kittridge Anne Mahoney is in a state of shock. It isn't until Joseph mews that Kitt comes around. The breaking of the mother's trance by her newborn's cry is a thing to behold.

Without word, Kitt takes her boy from Fred, and buzzes the babe's cheeks as she makes her way to his nursery. She talks her "momma-talk" while she checks his diaper, then sends him off to sleep with a slightly off-key rendition of *Golden Slumbers*. When she joins Fred in the master suite, she finds him stretched out on the bed, his back leaning against the headboard, his feet crossed at the ankles, and *that* Fred Serpico smile spread wide across his face. He's holding the baby monitor in his hand. "That whole Momma-Baby moment was a memory maker. I'm loving you beyond my capacity, Kittridge."

The very happy woman scoots onto the bed, taps Fred's thighs so he spreads them, crawls into the V and tucks her legs beneath her. She folds her forearms under her ample breasts.

Fred groans.

Kitt snickers. "Fred. Focus. Eyes up here." She snaps her fingers.

He smiles wide.

"Fred, I'm going to repeat what you told me. Please stop me if I run afoul, okay?"

His eyes drop a bit. "Right – stop – afoul."

Kitt snaps her fingers again. "Pay attention." She inches toward Fred, pulls herself to her full kneeling height, and begins, "You just told me that Joy did not die last October."

"Yes."

"Then that means that she isn't buried in a grave at the top of a small hill at Mayflower-Falls Cemetery. Please answer in an affirmative or a negative."

"Yes."

"I want you to tell me more of what's going on, but I have a question."

"Okay, shoot."

"Do you remember when we went to the funeral home to make arrangements for Joy, and we were told that the next of kin requested a burial only?"

Fred hitches up a bit against the headboard. "I'd forgotten about that. Why are you bringing it up?"

"We never had a viewing of Joy. The funeral director said that the casket was already sealed for burial. Do you remember that I was really upset because Joy got shot – was taken to the hospital – was taken to surgery – was taken to the morgue – was taken to the funeral home, and through it all she was alone? John was missing in action, and we couldn't ask him anything, and we didn't really have authority to demand anything..."

Fred interrupts. "So when the funeral director said, 'next of kin' we just assumed it was John. It wasn't John who made that call. Hell, it wasn't even Joy in the casket."

"Do you think someone is in that casket?" Kitt shivers. "And if so, who's in that casket?"

So, you don't have DOA?

John doesn't make it to bed that night. He stays at the barn working on his defense systems, and when he is sure that he's protected himself from cyber snoops, he makes a list and a plan—then he cautions himself. "Get into Gaffney's system. Find out every fucking thing there is to know about the 'deceased' Joy Ann Watts—then get the fuck out." *The deceased Joy Ann Watts*. The words get stuck in his head as she moves back into his heart, and he moves toward slumber.

D is for Dublin

He was waiting for her at the bus terminal when she arrived back in Dublin, actually, he'd been waiting for hours. "What's in County Monaghan?"

"Spying on me, John?"

"Didn't need to spy Joy, you're on public transportation."

"What I do with my time isn't for public consumption."

He took hold of her hand to stop her, "Joy, what's in County Monaghan?"

"John, I'm trying to row my boat, please don't rock it."

"What the fuck, Joy?"

She pulled her hand away. She started to say something, chose something else to say, "O, stony grey soil is in Country Monaghan."

"What's Patrick Kavanaugh got to do with this?"

She walked away.

"Joy!"

He startles awake.

Washington, DC

Director Gaffney didn't bother going to bed. He knew he wouldn't be getting any sleep that night, or any other for that matter—not with Joy Ann Watts still in the wind. "She should be back in my hands. I gave The Realm associate everything he needed for success."

"Wait until DOA contacts John Maxwell— when they separate, take her. If you see her before their meeting, grab her. It would be better if Maxwell doesn't learn that Watts is alive, but I doubt you'll get eyes on her before she makes contact with him. She's that good."

Gaffney's plan would have worked if there hadn't been another person with eyes on Joy Ann Watts.

"Gaffney, did you send a second tail?"

"No. Why?"

"I had eyes on Maxwell from the moment he stepped off the plane in Paris. I picked up Watts as she moved toward a café—the one he'd been sitting at for hours. I was about to grab her when this other dude stepped out of nowhere and started trailing her. He's not one of your agents?"

"No."

"Yeah. He didn't look like one of your people. He's probably a PI."

"So you don't have DOA?"

"No. I followed her to the café, the PI dude followed me to the café, we both watched Watts approach Maxwell. She said a few words to the stupefied man, and walked away. He stayed at the café for a minute or so, then started looking for her. The PI and I were already following her, but she fucking vanished, like a ghost. I wouldn't have been able to take her then, anyway."

"I fucking told you! If you didn't get Watts the first go-around, there wouldn't be a second. Make sure you let The Body know that this fuckup isn't on me!"

Gaffney stewed a bit that night, he is stewing a bit now. "The Realm associate followed Maxwell for days thinking he'd lead him to Joy. Maxwell fucking made that amateur, then he played him. The PI wasn't anywhere near Maxwell or the associate. **That's** the guy who had Watts in his sights. Whoever **that** guy is, he probably still has her in his sights." Gaffney picks up his phone. "Shea, she's still in the wind. The associate got elbowed out by some other guy on her tail. Find out who he is. He's probably a PI from the states, and probably arrived in Nice around August 1." There's a pause before Gaffney starts again. "Anything on Maxwell?"

"Nope."

"He hasn't been deep?"

"Nope."

"Of course he has. He must have built a wall. Find it and tear it down, Shea. I want to know every keystroke that bastard makes."

All I need to do is get there.

Joy wakes on Plage du Midi, a public beach on the western side of Cannes, located near the city's old quarter. She calls attention as she splashes at the water's edge in her shorts and sports bra, makes sure she is noticed at the beautiful public park, La Croix-des-Gardes, and all along the busy, friendly streets of Le Suquet. "I want people to notice me—I need them to tell my tail that I've been here. That way he'll have to invest some time in Cannes looking for me." She smiles at those who walk past and wonder at the mumbling woman.

After a second stroll through the park, Joy heads to a local café, and orders from inside, "Croissant and orange juice, to go, please." She tucks both into her satchel, and heads to the restroom. She removes her black wig, runs her cropped blonde hair under the faucet and finger-dries it under the wall-mounted hand dryer. When the former Special Agent steps back onto the streets of Le Suquet, she looks like Joy Ann Watts—and Joy Ann Watts is ready to take back her life. She goes directly to the Trenitalia train service that connects Cannes to several cities. She purchases a one-way ticket to Genoa, the G on the super-spies alphabetical reunion list. "I need help with my next plan. I have help in Genoa. All I need to do is get there."

Sainte Marguerite to Cannes

The private investigator wakes at the base of a beach retaining wall that runs the edge of a patio bar he helped close the night before. He is in the same foul mood as when he stepped off the ferry, and onto the dock at Sainte Marguerite. That's when he learned that the Amanda Seyfried lookalike boarded a ferry "off the island – headed to Cannes" only moments before his arrival. The dock workers directed the very pissed PI to the patio bar. It is the only place he's been since he arrived at Sainte Marguerite.

Bettke doesn't bother having breakfast. He heads directly to the docks and boards the first ferry to Cannes. As the commuter boat nears the Mediterranean commune of the rich and famous, he gets the feeling that he is on to something. "Waif woman is here, I can feel it, and I will find her. Of course, if I find her, all I can do is watch her. Boss lady said no contact of any kind." Bettke still doesn't know who he is following or why he is following her. He laughs as he makes his way from the docks. "Maybe I'm following Amanda Seyfried," the semi-inebriated PI jokes.

Cannes to Genoa

Joy boards the afternoon Thello at Trenitalia train service. Her scheduled arrival in Genoa is 6 PM. She sits back expecting to put her thoughts toward the future. Instead, her mind drifts back...

"She's critically wounded," the EMT said.

She felt pressure on her chest—struggled to breathe. She moved her hand—or did someone else move it? *Is someone holding my hand? Kitt is with me.* The thought comforted her.

"We're losing her."

She struggled to push words into the chaos. "John do list pink and white go deep Kitt thank you save Tess Fred message sorry save list Annie system crashed."

"Stay with us. Come on, Watts, stay with us."

"She's been out for a week. What makes you think she's even still in there?"

Joy is pulled from her dream by a conductor's announcement that the train is arriving at its destination. She gets off the train, checks to make sure she hasn't been followed, then places a call from a burner phone as she strolls the passageways of Genoa. While she waits through the phone's ringing, she imagines Cepriano Batista moving lithely through his apartment to answer the gilded cradle phone that sits upon a 19th-century marble-topped, intricately carved console table. Cep, as Joy was instructed to call him when they first met, does not own a cell phone, or a computer, or even a television for that matter. Cep enjoys a simple life—as simple a life as a legendary jewel thief can live, that is.

Cepriano Batista is a dashing older man with cropped silver hair, black brows, observant dark eyes, and a set of dimples that charmed the panties off many an ingénue in his day. His slight frame is still lean and toned, and perfect for his once-chosen profession. It is well-documented that the retired jewel thief wined and dined with the rich and famous, and European royalty for decades. The Master, as he was widely referred to, spent most of his life in villas and casinos, on yachts and jets of the upper strata of the French and Italian Rivieras. It mattered not to his hosts and hostesses that Cepriano was renowned in his jewel thievery; the elite wanted to rub elbows with the famed master—even when he made off with rarified gems the upper crust mistakenly deemed untouchable. Most society mavens did not demand justice; they considered it an honor to be a chapter in Batista's story. Those who wanted their pound of flesh, received it off the backs of Cep's loyal man-servants—men who willingly provided the ultimate service to their employer by sitting in jail cells along the Mediterranean. When The Master retired, it was to a pink building in the multi-hued seaside neighborhood of Boccadasse. He lives quietly in his gilded apartment with his assistant Dieci, the tenth loyalist to serve him.

"I wonder if Cep has heard of my death." Joy whispers as the phone continues to ring. All it takes for Cepriano to know it is Joy on the line is her one word greeting, "Cep."

"Gia, it is you! I knew rumors of your death were evil tales. I felt it in my heart and soul, my caro, Gia."

Joy wishes she could stay on the line forever, but they need to keep the call short. She tells Cep what she needs, and he agrees to help.

"Meet me at the fountain at Piazza de Ferrari tomorrow at 10 AM. Dress chic, Gia," he ends the call by giving her an address and an appointment time.

The weary traveler spends the night wandering the medieval labyrinth of streets and alleyways of Genoa. When she can walk no further, she sets her duffle into the corner of a doorway, puts herself upon it, and gets some shuteye.

G is for Genoa

"What did you do today?" she asked before landing a quick peck to his cheek.

He pulled her close, and kissed her as though he hadn't seen her or touched her in years. It had only been hours since they went their own ways on the streets of Genoa. "I walked Via Garibaldi, checked out a few palaces, and museums. The usual. What did you do?"

"I met a jewel thief at the pebble beach in Boccadasse," her smile owning every inch of her face.

"Of course you did. Cepriano Batista, I presume."

"You presume correctly. Do you know, Cep?"

"Of him."

"Of course you do."

He smirked then moved her to their bed and kissed her as though he hadn't seen her or touched her in years.

Seattle

Roni wakes in the middle of the night and checks her phone. There are three missed calls from the private investigator. She returns his call, not knowing, or caring, what time it is, wherever he is. "You called."

"Yeah. Thought you might want to know she's in the wind. I'm coming back."

It's a Federal offense, but whatever.

After a pre-dawn run up Farm Road High, and down Farm Road low, and back again, John Maxwell showered, grabbed something to eat, and headed to the barn. He sat at his terminal and readied himself for the task at hand— hacking the systems of FICA Director, Roland Gaffney. "It's a Federal offense, but whatever..." For more than a decade John Maxwell, aka Sam Sawyer, set and maintained Director Gaffney's cyber security. When he enters the space, he sees that it's been changed. "Looks like my days at J. Edgar are numbered." The agent smirks—the veritable genius rears his arrogant head as he maneuvers through the newly erected defense system. "Let's see what you've got, newbie...not bad, not bad. An opening? You left an opening? I am the preeminent defender of cyberland. I can take down any system in the world, asshole newbie. All this proves is that Gaffney wants me in his space OR he's laying a trap, and I just sprung it."

The cyber defender-turned-hunter goes where no one should go uninvited, into Gaffney's cyberspace. He grabs what he wants, then pulls out. "The courtesy opening into Gaffney's system isn't about **my** access—it's so whoever is monitoring the cyberspace can see when I go in, what I do while I'm in, and what I take on the way out." The Special Agent in him wants to look around, if only to see which FICA agent is monitoring him—he quickly reminds himself, "Don't tip your hand. You're supposed to be searching for Joy, and investigating Roni, nothing else."

After rummaging through Gaffney's system Special Agent Maxwell goes deep. He picks up a tail for his troubles. When he's sure he's lost the annoyance, he finds and opens a file he deposited into cyberspace years ago— the one his boss asked him to "deep six". John never opened the file before—he never had a reason to. "Things change, Roland. This file's been floating for so long, I almost forgot about it. Looks like you did too." He opens the file, and gets the confirmation he needs. "Gaffney knew from Day One that Joy and Roni stayed in contact after Joy went Dead On Assignment." The file has another tidbit of information. "Heads at the CIA, DEA, Homeland Security, and British Intelligence were told that FICA had an agent Dead on Assignment. That makes sense." He thinks things through a bit. "What doesn't make sense is that they were given her identity markers and part of her backstory. Per Agency protocol, that information should have been cloaked. What the fuck, Roland? Any one of these individuals could have outed her, intentionally or not. It's a miracle that Hector – or – DOA's legions of enemies couldn't find her from the get-go." He shakes his head in disgust. "The MFPD detectives' jobs just got way more complicated. Eleven suspects has increased exponentially. Current directors. Former directors. Interim directors. Acting directors. None of them should have known who DOA was…who she is."

The cyber diver thinks about surfacing, but decides to take one more pass through Gaffney's files—he finds a shiny new embedded object—a little something left by someone other than the newbie defender. "Huh. A little tidbit left by the Director, himself. A notation about the FICA agent who investigated Special Agent John Maxwell. He **wants** me to know?"

The cyber snoop reads the name, quickly surfaces, and slumps back in his chair. "Agent Dan Shea. Fucking Dan Shea!" John leans forward, puts his elbows onto his knees, and drops his face into his shaking hands. He needs to calm himself or he will tear Netti Barn the fuck apart. Memories bang in his tortured mind, reopen wounds that haven't rightly healed. He sits for hours. By the time he works through his shit, he is pissed enough to make a call he shouldn't make.

"Dad. It's 7 AM."

"Too early?"

"Nope, I was already up."

"You're a liar, Annie," he pokes.

"Do you want to be the pot or the kettle?" she jabs.

"Pot. Always the pot. Look, can you come to Netti Barn?"

"Sure. When?"

"Now."

Annie leans over and kisses Mike on the cheek. "I'm going to Netti. Stay in bed. I shouldn't be long."

Like a thief in the night.

Despite the cramped quarters and slumped position, Joy falls into a bone-crushing sleep of the dead—though her mind is wreaking havoc on her, pushing free, fragments from her time in captivity…

"She's been out for a week. What makes you think she's even still in there or will be able to work again?"

"To you she is sleeping. To me she is working her way back. Be patient."

She woke sometime later, perhaps days, maybe weeks. Her eyes fell upon the back of a tall, black man with long dreads. He was wearing a long white doctor's coat, dungarees, and Birkenstocks. She cleared her throat, and the man turned from the window.

He smiled wide and introduced himself from across the room. "My name is Jason Bennett, Ms. Watts. I have been taking care of you while you rested from your ordeal. May I approach?"

She nodded at the smiling, hippy dude.

He checked her vitals, staring into her eyes frequently, gauging her level of awareness. He quietly gave her time to adjust. He said nothing, yet saw everything. Before he was finished with her exam, she had drifted off to sleep.

The doorway vagrant is roused early by a boy running past her as though he's being chased by the Devil. Joy quickly moves from the duffle beneath her and follows the deep smell of espresso to a sidewalk café. After two thick jolts in a cup, she goes in search of the boutique Cep told her to find, the one with black and white doors on Via XX Settembre. She arrives a few minutes before its opening so she meanders the shopper's alleyway, peeking here and there, then stopping to look through the window of a nearby art gallery. Interesting tri-color paintings framed in matte black line the walls. A beautiful brown, white, and blue ceramic wall of mosaic that is chipped in several places, is prominently showcased in the middle of the gallery. "Why is that beautiful piece cracked and why are several of the squared sections missing? Broken art? Is that such a thing?" She steps back and reads the name hanging on the gallery. "Fiancetti." She hears a door open and close behind her and makes her way to the now-open boutique.

A magnificent woman with waist-length black hair and cerulean blue eyes smiles as Joy enters the shop. The goddess is at least 6' tall and is wearing a white satin tube top and sheer black palazzo pants. She is barefoot, and the middle toe of her left foot has a gold ring with a chain that travels up the top of the foot and wraps around her ankle. Joy is roused from her fascination with the beguiling woman...

"Gia, come with me."

Joy follows through a curtained area and within minutes, "Carlotta" has stripped, washed, dressed, and transformed the homeless spy. It is in the stripping and washing that Joy becomes self-aware, and tense.

Carlotta dips her head ever so slightly when she sees Joy's scars. She holds Joy's eyes steady and shows deference to the woman's victory over death. "You carry them well, Gia."

Joy's eyes sting with tears, but she keeps them for herself and packs them back where they belong. She turns toward a framed standing mirror, and stares at the beautifully dressed and coiffed woman staring back. Exhaling on a sigh she whispers, "If Cep wanted me chic, then that's what he is getting."

Carlotta smiles, "Si, Gia." The women embrace and go back to their worlds.

Joy Ann Watts, Cepriano Batista's dress up doll, leaves Bianco e Nero boutique decked boho chic from head to toe. Her dress is a sleeveless brick floral V-neck, cut deep to mid-torso. It is hi-lo hemmed, the high hitting mid-shin, the low hitting her ankles which are wrapped several times with the leather straps of four-inch wedged sandals. Her cropped blonde hair is tucked under a straw fedora that matches a round straw bag draped messenger style across her chest. Her belongings are now in a fashionable leather valise that she carries with ease. Joy smiles at the heads that turn her way as she nears the fountain at Piazza de Ferrari. As she did in Cannes, she flaunts herself, making sure the people and street cameras in Genoa capture her image. She will be gone from Genoa in a matter of minutes, so she gives the eyes that follow her something interesting for their troubles.

At 10 AM on the dot, Cepriano Batista and his assistant, Dieci, join the super-chic super-spy at the fountain. "Bella, Gia, such wonders you are," he enthuses as he approaches.

The friends embrace. It is not one of expectation, but of resignation. They know, or fear, that this moment may be the end of their time together. Cep pulls back and gently wipes a solitary tear that slips from Joy's eye. "Caro, Gia, you mustn't weep. You are alive, sì?"

Joy gently squeezes Cep's hand. "Sì, my dear friend."

A third man joins them at the fountain, quietly interrupting the moment. He is casually dressed in black slacks, a white button-down shirt cuffed under to the elbow, and black loafers sans socks. The man is beautifully Italian – black closely cropped hair, graying slightly at the temples, deep dark eyes that seem way too knowing, and a carefully trimmed scruff that barely hides dimples that are unneeded as his smile can easily melt a woman's panties.

Joy leans into Cep. "I don't know why I'm telling you this, but I'm not wearing panties. Carlotta wouldn't let me."

Cepriano laughs as he puts his hand to Joy's cheek. "Just as well, Gia. Your escort has panty-melting abilities. I wouldn't want you to get singed."

Joy laughs at their kindred thoughts and notices Dieci's outermost lips lift into a seldom-seen smile as he looks away.

Cep introduces the Italian Stallion. "Gia, this is your husband, Rocco Fiancetti."

"As in the art gallery on Via XX Settembre?" Joy asks.

"Sì, my Papa's." The escort gets down to business. "These are for you." He hands her Italian citizen papers, a passport, and itinerary for a British Airways flight from Genoa's Cristoforo Colombo Airport to London's Heathrow. "From there, we fly to Toronto. I am your protection, Signora Fiancetti, until I say otherwise. Sì?"

Joy nods.

Rocco bows slightly, takes hold of her hand, and slips a simple gold band onto her left ring finger. He unburdens her of her valise and kisses both of her cheeks. "Il mio amore, Gia, we should leave for our flight, sì?"

Joy nods to her new husband and turns to thank Cepriano Batista, but he is gone like a thief in the night.

You shouldn't trust me.

Mr. and Mrs. Fiancetti nestle into their first-class seats and quietly prove that they are in love. The husband whispers sweet nothings into his wife's ear, nibbles, and kisses along the hand he holds tightly in his, strokes the shiny, new wedding band with his thumb, and looks longingly into her dazzling blues.

Joy mumbles as she turns her head toward the window, "If I had panties, they'd be s.m.o.k.i.n.g."

The husband leans near. "Ripetere, Gia," then kisses her knuckles – one – by – one.

The wife shakes her head, and leans back into her seat. She closes her eyes for several minutes, then opens them to a gentle kiss on her cheek.

"Mi, amore. Don't respond to my words. Only my touch, si?"

Joy nods and snuggles close to the magnificent man canoodling her.

"It is my honor to escort the preeminent cyber huntress known as DOA."

Joy responds. She locks his hand in a bone-crushing squeeze.

"Ow, mi amore, relax," he tries to pull his hand away, he fails. "I am British Intelligence, Senior Special Operative, Rocco Fiancetti, although I do have other aliases. But for now I work for Cepriano Batista, my uncle. He confided in me years ago that he met the huntress of the deepest realm. It is through him that I am aware of your happily untrue death. Today, and for the next many, I work for Uncle Cep. I will get you into Heathrow and out of Heathrow tonight. You will do what I say, when I say. Is that clear, Special Agent Watts?"

Joy releases his hand, shifts in her seat and looks directly at her escort. "How do I know I can trust you?"

Rocco Fiancetti leans in and places a kiss on Joy's lips and traces it away with the pad of his thumb. "You shouldn't trust me, Gia, but you *can* trust Cepriano Batista."

The changeover at Heathrow goes off without a hitch. Once again, Mr. and Mrs. Fiancetti nestle into their first-class seats. An hour into their flight across the pond, Joy closes her eyes and drifts back into that dream…

She woke sometime later, perhaps days, maybe weeks. Her eyes fell upon the back of a tall, black man with long dreads. He was wearing a long white doctor's coat, dungarees, and Birkenstocks. She cleared her throat, and the man turned from the window.

He approached her, this time without asking if he could. He checked her vitals. "You have questions?"

She nodded.

"Are you able to speak, Ms. Watts?"

"Yes," she croaked.

"And you know who you are?"

"DOA," she said

He smiled and gave her a shot.

Joy wakes with a start, her heart is racing, and a panic has been released by her dream – by the memories they hold. Her need to leave her seat is eased only by her pretend husband who has her hand in his. He gently squeezes it. "You dream of bad things, Gia." Her "husband" touches her cheek, "Mi amore, you are truly beautiful, too beautiful to have lived the lonely life of a cyber ghost."

Joy looks out the darkened window at darkened nothingness and closes her eyes to darkened thoughts and dreams...

She woke. Her eyes automatically turned toward the window. The man with dreads and the white doctor coat was standing there—he was always standing there. "Are you a doctor?"

He turned toward her; that comforting smile of his already on his face. "Why do you ask?"

"You are always here."

"You are my only patient, Ms. Watts."

"Where am I? Why hasn't anyone come to see me?"

"You are at a secure medical facility." When the man moved toward her, he let her see that he was armed.

"Are you FBI?"

He smiled. "Do you remember the events at Netti Barn?"

"I was shot...by Hector."

"Yes. You were critically wounded. You are in protective custody because you were unmasked."

"No. No. No," she said before he gave her a shot.

Joy thrashes in her seat, "No. No. No."

Rocco touches her shoulder. "Gia, you need to wake."

She struggles to orient herself. Her racing heart begins to slow, her focus returns to the man next to her, and to the reason they are together. "They want me."

Rocco makes no acknowledgement of her words. "Gia. We will land in Toronto within minutes and immediately board a private jet to the States. If we get separated, my men will get you to the jet. Get on that jet." Rocco presses a piece of paper into her hand. "Follow the instructions on this paper. Do not improvise. Follow them explicitly."

Joy turns back to the dark expanse beyond the tiny window. "They want me."

The Fiancettis are met by two "Fiancetti" men when they deplane at Toronto Pearson International Airport. The men are dressed in black T-shirts, jeans, Doc Martens, and leather bomber jackets. They flank the newlyweds and bob and weave them through the airport terminal. The spies are quickly led to a door at the far end of the concourse, behind which is an escalator that ends in the airport basement. They exit out onto the tarmac, where a Learjet 45XR sits ready for takeoff.

The British Intelligence Officer ushers the former FICA Special Agent onto the jet. The captain and first-officer are already on board, and seated in the cockpit. Nods, but no words, are exchanged as the travelers move further into the plane. The configuration of the interior has seats on either side of an aisle. Rocco moves Joy past the first front-facing row of seats toward the next section with a front- and rear-facing seat configuration. He has her sit facing the front of the jet. "Gia, we will liftoff soon."

She is deep in thought.

"You should buckle, si."

She is lost in thought.

He reaches across and buckles her, then takes the seat across from her. The energy inside the jet is tense. Rocco remains leaning forward, listening intently to the crew's communication with air traffic control, and assessing the woman seated near. When the jet begins its taxi toward liftoff, he buckles himself and relaxes into his seat. At cruising altitude, he unbuckles, leans toward Joy, and lifts her hand. He presses a kiss on her palm and another on her pulse point. He feels it quicken. He holds his kiss for several seconds. The warmth of his lips is intense—branding. She finds, then stares into her escort's eyes, quickly remembers that they belong to an international spy.

"Welcome back, Gia. You were deep in reflections." He inches forward, their knees touch, their hands entwine. He stares intently at her face, her exquisite face. Her eyes hold uncertainty, yet invite passion. He is intrigued by this woman—a problem for them both. The spy, the hired escort, leans back into his seat and tries to quell his attraction. It doesn't work. He wants to know this woman. "Gia, will you play a game with me? A twenty question game. I want to know you before you are back in the wind."

"Spies don't ask questions. They find answers," she quips.

"Ah, but I want to see you as you open yourself to me, Gia."

"Five questions each," she consents with a haughty nod.

"Ladies first," he encourages with a slight bow of his head. "All questions must be answered—unless national security prevails," he smiles w.i.d.e.

"Why British Intelligence?" she charges in.

"The British part of my answer is that my mother was British. The Intelligence part of my answer is that I wanted to be a spy, James Bond, actually," he smiles wide, his dimples running his face and setting his dark eyes with mischief.

Joy chuckles and shakes her head.

He kisses her hand before asking his first question, "You were so deep for so long, did you not crave a man's touch?"

"No." She pauses a moment, before asking her second question. "How did Cepriano learn that I am DOA?"

"I have no clue how my uncle knows such things." He smiles and adds, "Some things are better of the not knowing, si?"

She nods, "si."

"My turn. You fight to get home. What is waiting there for you, bella, Gia?"

She scoffs. "Honestly, what waits for me may be nothing more than a fantasy I conjured up in a pink and white room one night."

Rocco doesn't understand—he is not meant to understand.

Joy asks another question. "What is your age, Rocco? I think you are my contemporary, but you have Cep's bloodline. So who knows?"

"Tell me, Gia, how old do you think Uncle Cep is?"

"I don't know, somewhere between 100 and 150."

Rocco laughs big. His eyes get into the action, all twinkling with amazement and amusement. "Oh, you are special, Gia. My uncle, I do not know his age. As for myself I am not your contemporary unless you are fifty. If you are fifty you have a very good bloodline." The man leans in, "I believe it is my turn. Tell me, are you wearing panties?"

She raises a brow. "Carlotta dressed me, so what do you think?"

"If Carlotta dressed you, then the answer is no. He does not approve of undergarments."

"He?" she astonishes.

Rocco laughs loud and long. "You did not know?"

Joy laughs loud and long. "Apparently, I owe you two answers, Mr. Fiancetti. No, I am not wearing panties. And no I did not know Carl was a man." Joy doesn't skip a beat before asking her next question. "Is Rocco Fiancetti your real name?"

"Si, although I have several assumed names, and a second name of register in the U.K."

"Continue with your answer, Mister…"

"Duff, Alistair Duff," he bows his head. "It is a pleasure to make your acquaintance, Ms. Watts," he says in a perfect upper crust British accent.

Joy snickers. "No wonder your preference is the Italian Rocco."

"And is that your preference, Gia, the Italian Rocco?"

"Is that one of your questions?"

"Si," he smiles.

"Si," she smiles. "I believe we have come to the last round of questions."

He nods. "So we have."

Joy surprises herself when she asks, "Are you married?"

"If I told you that I am not married, Gia, would you believe me?"

Joy locks onto his eyes. "You told me not to trust you, Mr. Fiancetti, but I will believe what you tell me. An important decision is upon you, sì?"

He nods and smiles. "I am not married, mi amore." Rocco Fiancetti takes a knee in front of Joy Ann Watts. He runs his fingers through her hair. "I believe my next question will be the last of this game." He kisses her lips then locks onto her eyes. "Gia, before our time together ends, will you let me pleasure you?"

Joy surprises herself again. "Sì."

He sits back onto his seat and extends his hand. She leans into his pull and nestles onto his lap. Joy lets Rocco pleasure her, reducing her to a boneless puddle. The super-chic super-spy suddenly gets the appeal of going without panties.

"Thank you, Carl."

"Gia, you are a delight."

What crawled up your butt?

The preeminent cyber huntress is still in the wind, and The Body is losing his patience. He has made that point abundantly clear.

"Roland, things seem to have stalled."

"I'm not the one to blame for the fuckups."

"This conversation isn't about assigning blame, it is about expressing my concerns."

"Things are starting to move along. Maxwell took the bait. He visited my cyberspace, and snooped in a file that was suspended years ago."

"What's in the file?"

"A confirmed connection between Joy Ann Watts and Veronica Shields."

"And?"

"A bit of finger-pointing toward people who know about DOA, and her background. He's going to want to know if any of them outed her, and if any of them are helping her."

"And?"

"We let him do our work, follow along, and beat him to the punch."

"This better work, Roland."

Gaffney got a reprieve, but he needs to find Joy Ann Watts and smuggle her back to the United States—quickly! Chatter has begun that DOA isn't dead. The FICA director didn't share

that bit of information with The Body. "What he doesn't know won't hurt him. What he does know could very well hurt me." Gaffney gets back to monitoring the chatter which is still confined to the abyss, "Not many people are involved in the speculative conversation, but the ones who think something is afoul, are the ones who present the greatest danger. If a foreign entity gets DOA, then she will be forced to work against the interests of The Realm and The Body—if she lives long enough to work, that is."

Gaffney's focused energy turns on a dime, he becomes enraged about the mistakes that have been made. "Joy going on the run isn't on me." He slams his hand on his desk. Once. Twice. "Secure medical facility my ass! The fuckup in Nice isn't on me, either. The associate that The Body sent to get the cyber huntress isn't an Agency man, he works for The Realm. Still, it is a setback – one that's wasting time and money – one that's shining a bad light on me. I'm the one who told The Body he could have DOA. It was my entrance fee into The Realm." He moves beyond his anger and takes stock of his life now that he's turned a corner and ended up on the dark side. "This is all my doing. If I hadn't... For fuck's sake, Roland, there is no going back from this—for you or anyone else associated with The Body. Work the fucking problem and get DOA!"

The Director of FICA logs back onto his system and checks his cyber files. "Come on, Maxwell, pull the stuff you need and find out where the fuck Joy Ann Watts is, so I can get her, and deal with you. Depending on how things shake out, you'll either end up in solitary confinement at some supermax penitentiary, or six fucking feet under."

Netti

Annie is smiling wide, her long hair swishing back and forth as she bounds into the barn. Her smile fades quickly. "Well, you look awful. What crawled up your butt and dug in sideways?"

Unlike others in his immediate circle, when John Maxwell looks at his oldest daughter, he never sees poodle-Annie, he only sees pit bull-Annie. He expects to see the ferocious canine at any moment. "I have news. Do you want it straight up or sugarcoated?"

"Sugarcoating is for breakfast cereals. Give it to me straight, Dad."

"Joy Ann Watts is alive."

No more than three beats pass before Annie responds. "I know this should be shocking news, but nothing about your super-de-duper spy work is all that shocking anymore."

The father-daughter-duo smirk, then laugh.

An hour after John began telling Annie everything that's happened, she finally speaks. "So this is where I come in. You want me to be your cyber huntress." It isn't a question. It. Should. Be. A. Question.

"Yes."

"Strictly for clarification, Dad, you want me to infiltrate the FICA Director's systems to get information. Is that correct?"

"Yes."

"Is that a federal crime?"

"Yes."

"I need to make a call."

Seattle

Roni puts the last few things into her carry-on and zips it tight. She does a quick once-over of her place then heads out the door. Her Uber is waiting at the curb when she exits her high-rise. She summarily waves off the driver's help with her bag, and gets in.

On the drive to Sea-Tac Airport, Roni bangs her brains bloody with questions that have no answers, and suppositions that are baseless. Still, she continues the frontal lobe assault until she takes her first-class seat—and her first pull of tequila. She quickly does some math, "This is a three hundred and ninety minute flight, if I have one nip every eighty minutes that will register an approximate 0.050 BAC, so..." She raises her empty tumbler toward the first flight attendant who comes her way, "I'll want four more of these, then cut me off."

"Yes, Ms. Shields."

I fucking walked away.

Fred and Steve arrive at the spy headquarters of John Maxwell—a place that may very well become a murder scene. Again.

"Annie's Jeep!" Steve.

"What the fuck?" Fred.

"Oh, shit, no!" Both.

Fred nearly pulls off the door of Netti Barn. "John! Tell me Annie isn't part of this!"

Annie nudges her father. "Told you he'd freak."

Fred points to Annie. "You don't speak." Then he points to John. "You, speak."

John moves toward Fred. "I'm not a hunter. I am a defender. I can penetrate walls and get shit, but Annie can go chasing it. This investigation needs the best huntress there is and right now that's Annie. I did some cyber snooping last night and found out some things, but I'm not the best resource for the work that needs to be done, Fred. The stakes are too high to limit ourselves to me hunting in Gaffney's and FICA's systems." He takes a breath and makes his plea. "Let's go to the farmhouse, and I'll tell you what I know so far. Then we will all decide about Annie."

Fred hates that Annie knows about Joy almost as much as he hates being in the damn cave. And yet, Annie knows about Joy, and he is in the damn cave. "Well, this day sucks, already. You may as well top it off, John."

The Special Agent takes some wall space. "Before I even got into Director Gaffney's system, it was obvious that he wanted me there. He has a new security defender who left an opening in the defense wall so I could get in. First, that fucking pisses me off. I'm the best defender in the fucking world. I know how to bring down a wall. To top that shit off, Gaffney's new security defender is Agent Dan Shea."

John pauses.

The others ponder.

Fred looks at Steve, who looks at Annie, who looks at Fred. All of them shrug their shoulders. "Are we supposed to know who Dan Shea is?" Fred asks.

"Nope. But he's quickly becoming one of the most interesting characters in this mess. First, he is the agent Gaffney assigned to investigate and surveil me and Roni in New York. I learned that because Gaffney went in and embedded that kernel of information into one of the cyber files I pulled from his cyberspace. I would have figured out Dan Shea did the investigation and surveillance eventually, but for some reason Gaffney was eager for me to know it. Now for the interesting part..."

Steve jumps in, "I don't know about anyone else, but I think what you already told us is pretty damn interesting."

"Not even close to being interesting, Steve. When I arrived at Mayflower-Falls Regional after the shooting at Netti Barn, a man approached me outside the Emergency department. He introduced himself as Agent Dan Shea. He said he was part of a field team dispatched that morning by Gaffney. He said the team was a medical unit and that it transported Special Agent Watts to Mayflower-Falls Medical, and that she was under guard in the OR. When I asked how she was, he said that she was in critical condition. Now skip ahead to when we were at the surgical unit waiting area and a surgical nurse had just told Fred about Mike's condition. Out of the corner of my eye, I caught sight of FBI Agent Shea. He started walking toward me, his eyes locked onto mine, and his head began shaking back and forth. I read all of that to mean that Joy had died. I was sure I knew what he was going to say so instead of waiting to hear it, I walked away. I fucking walked away. I never made him tell me that Joy was dead. Maybe if I'd made him tell me…" John is so pissed he is physically shaking.

As are the other three "cave dwellers".

Fred claps his hands, and jumps in. "Okay. I want to dissect Dan Shea's conversation with John because it sort of wraps with the questions I had about Gaffney sending Agency help the morning of the shooting. Let me recap all of that for Annie. Before I start, let me just say for the record that I really wanted to raise my son, but that seems unlikely once Kittridge finds out Annie is part of this. As sure as I'm sitting in this godforsaken cave, Kittridge Anne Mahoney is going to have my godforsaken hide."

The three dwellers nod their agreement.

Fred claps his hands and gets back to work. "Gaffney told John that one hour before the shooting, Joy crashed her FICA systems in keeping with FICA protocol when an undercover agent is unmasked. Gaffney said that when he was alerted to DOA's system crash, he put agents in the field to find her and bring her in 'for her protection'. The agents he sent were part of a medically trained FICA unit who worked on Joy in the ambulance, during a med-flight, and at a secure medical facility. My first question, Annie, was how did Gaffney get agents to Netti Barn as quickly as he did? From the time we left the bungalow, to the time of Joy's shooting, it couldn't have been more than two hours. That's not a lot of time..." Fred stops when he sees the look on Annie's face. "Shit." He goes and squats in front of the young woman who he thinks of as a daughter. He takes her hands in his, "I'm so sorry, Annie, those two hours must have felt like an eternity to you. Are you sure you want to be here, listening to this, doing this?"

The young woman, the one Hector brought to an inch of her life, pulls a deep cleansing breath. "I'm sure, Fred. And don't sugarcoat things. I'll just work through them. Okay?"

"You got it, Pixie." He claps again. "I'm sure Gaffney has a ton of resources readily available, but no one could assemble a medical unit, get them outfitted as EMTs, into an ambulance, and to Netti Barn in two hours' time. I just isn't doable. Gaffney's plan—whatever it is—was already in motion…"

"Fred," John interrupts, "I've been thinking back to the conversation Joy and I had with Gaffney the night we were all at Bullet Bungalow, when Joy gave the Director the list of wannabe FICA agents to research. Gaffney said that he would send agents to Mayflower in case Hector showed up. If I'm remembering that conversation correctly, that would widen his window of time in getting his field agents ready and to Netti."

Fred nods. "I remembered that too, and after banging it about, it still doesn't explain the medically trained agents. When you and Joy were talking with Gaffney that night, no one knew Hector was in Mayflower. No one knew that he would take Annie the next morning and go to Netti for a standoff. And no one knew that DOA would crash her systems while sitting in her daughter's pink and white chevron bedroom. So when Gaffney told you and Joy that he'd send agents, what kind of agents was he planning to send?" Fred sprints toward the door. "There's a thread I need to pull. I'll be right back."

"Window," the cohorts laugh in unison.

Fred sprints back into the room several minutes later. "Got it," he smiles. "The night before the shooting, Gaffney said he was sending agents to help with the Hector case. The next morning he puts agents in the field to find Joy and bring her in, 'for her protection'. Jump ahead to the conversation Gaffney had with John at Logan—he said that when the team got to Joy, protection was secondary to saving her life. He said the medical team worked on her in the ambulance, during the med-flight, and at a secure medical facility. Why on God's earth did Gaffney arrange an ambulance, a med-flight, and a secure medical facility for an agent who hadn't been shot or injured in any way? Furthermore, if Gaffney thought Joy was in danger because of Hector and dispatched help for her—why didn't he do the same for John? Special Agent, John Maxwell, was in greater danger from Hector than anyone else. Yet, Gaffney was putting a team in place to provide protection for Joy. Listen up, boys and girls. I don't think Gaffney sent anyone to protect Joy Ann Watts. I think Gaffney planned on taking Joy Ann Watts. I think he had a medical team onsite at Netti Barn to drug her, kidnap her, and keep her. I don't know why, but we are gonna find the fuck out why."

Whoomph!

The Learjet taxis off the runway at Worcester Regional Airport, located in central Massachusetts. Rocco and Joy are ushered off the jet by the pilot and copilot and taken inside the near-empty terminal. They are met by two men dressed in the "I work for Rocco Fiancetti" trademark T-shirt, jeans, Doc Martens, and leather bomber jacket. They hand Rocco two duffle bags, and a set of car keys, then lead the couple to a private VIP conference room. A table and eight chairs sit in the middle of the room, and a bank of windows lines an entire wall. Rocco pulls closed the vertical blinds putting the room into near-darkness. He hands one of the duffle bags to Joy and leads her to one of two washrooms complete with standup shower, sink, and toilet. "Freshen up and change. You have ten minutes tops."

Joy nods and steps toward the washroom, turns back when Rocco calls her name. "Gia, if there are panties in that bag, leave them in that bag," he winks.

Joy is sitting at the conference room table dressed in the female version of the "I work for Rocco Fiancetti" uniform. Her jeans are tight and slung low, her T-shirt is white and form fitting, and her Doc Martens are of the shit-kicking variety. She is drumming her fingers on the table when Rocco enters from freshening up. "Took you long enough, sweetheart," she quips, as she examines the man in jeans, T-shirt, and Docs. She shivers. Twice.

The M.A.N. moves toward Joy the way a big cat stalks its prey. He drops his duffle onto the floor, takes hold of her chair, rolls it away from the table, and spins her toward him.

When the chair stops, Joy's face is Rocco-crotch high. She smirks. "Well, isn't this the 'in your face moment' to beat all others."

He pulls the W.O.M.A.N. from her seat making notice of the sexual excitement poking against her T-shirt. "Ah, you are taking Carlotta's advice about wearing as few clothings as possible, I see."

"You said no panties."

"Si, but I did not mention your brassiere, mi amore."

"The bra and panties are a matching set. I didn't want to separate them."

Rocco laughs at the woman he finds captivating. "Gia, you are such a delight."

The pretend newlyweds are in the conference room ten minutes times two orgasms. One for the Mister and one for the Missus.

The satisfied spies exit the terminal to a beautiful, sunny morning. From behind dark aviator shades, the Senior Special Operative does a panoramic scan of their surroundings. Aside from Fiancetti's men, they are alone. Rocco takes Joy's hand and leads her to a silver Mercedes GT Roadster parked at the curb. The two-seater beauty is exotic and expensive.

Joy eyes the car then nudges the MI6 Operative. "Well, this sure is in keeping with your James Bond fantasy," she smiles wide.

"As was the conference room dalliance, Pussy Galore," he smiles even wider.

Rocco key fobs the locks and steps to the trunk. He grabs a black duffle out, and puts their two duffles and Gia's valise in. He places his hand at the small of Joy's back and leads her to the passenger side door. She eases herself into luxury, "Mmmmm."

"Ah, a familiar sound," the lover winks. He leans in for a quick peck, and places the duffle on the floor next to her feet. "Don't kick this, it will kick back." When he shuts the door, it makes the most wonderful "whoomph" sound. After the second "whoomph" they are on their way.

"Where are we going?" Joy asks.

"To get your life back." With that, Rocco Fiancetti and Joy Ann Watts head to Mayflower.
Whoomph!

Netti
The decision is unanimous, albeit reluctantly so. Annie is on the case. The *Joy is Alive* taskforce is on their way to Netti Barn when Mike

Monopoli, Annie's lover and former MFPD officer arrives. Two detectives and a cyber spy stop dead in their tracks.

Annie keeps walking and sets everyone straight. "I'm on this investigation if you meet my terms. We tell Mike everything." Annie waves her hand at John, Fred, and Steve. "You three are secret keepers. I don't know if it's a disease, or maybe it has something to do with your generation, but I don't intend on keeping secrets from the man I love. Yes, gentlemen, I am in love with Michael whatever-his-middle-name-is Monopoli. And by the way Mike, I hadn't planned on telling you that I love you in this manner, but there you have it. I'm in love with you. Now, back to you other three, if you want my help, Mike comes along for the ride. The clock is ticking, so decide."

Michael whatever-his-middle-name-is Monopoli is the only man smiling—and he is smiling w.i.d.e.

DC

Gaffney is behind closed doors at J. Edgar, and very much behind the eight-ball. He pulls up the alphabetical reunion list John and Joy gave him when the cyber huntress went Dead On Assignment. He studies it for many minutes. "Maybe someone in Europe met you during one of your reunion trips and is helping you now. It was against protocol for you to make friendships or form alliances, but you broke that rule with Veronica Shields. I doubt that was a one-off." The Director studies the list, concentrating on European cities: Athens, Berlin, Dublin, Edinburgh, Florence, Genoa, Lisbon, Madrid, and Nice. He focuses on cities along the Mediterranean: Florence, Genoa, Lisbon, Madrid, and Nice.

He pulls a gulp of whiskey from a bottle he keeps hidden in his desk drawer. The amber liquor has been smoothing out the rough edges of his life for months. A euphemism, of course, for his oft-drunken state. He takes another long pull and complains, "I could use some help from my European counterparts, but they all think the preeminent cyber huntress is dead."

If the Director could, he would reach out to MI5 or MI6, Britain's equivalent to the FBI and CIA. But he's not willing to trust that FICA's supposed allies wouldn't try to get DOA into their own hands. "No. I'm going to have to deal with this mess alone." The frustrated man drops the list back into his system's cyberspace. "Maxwell will know I was looking at it. Let him figure out if she's with someone from the list. I'll just sit back and wait and when he finds her, I'll get her."

Before Gaffney shuts down his system, he drops in one more thing for John to find. A name. A private investigator's name: Bill Bettke.

Netti

The *Joy Is Alive* taskforce divides into two teams: John and Fred—Steve and Annie. As requested, Mike is along for the ride. John enters cyberland and heads directly to Gaffney's system. He finds two little gifts from the Director: the reunion list and the name, Bill Bettke. "This is ridiculous. He could have just given me this shit."

"Yeah, but then he wouldn't be able to bring you up on Federal charges for hacking his system."

"Us. Bring us up on Federal charges."

Fred shakes his head, "I'm not gonna be able to raise my boy, am I?"

"Don't worry, Kitt is really good with kids." John laughs. He's been doing that a lot lately—go figure.

Steve and Annie ignore the bullshit and continue their focus on their worldwide search for Bill Bettke—they hit paydirt. "There's a private investigator out of Seattle named Bill Bettke. I'd be willing to go all-in that he's gonna lead us to Roni," Steve says.

John connects Steve's assumption to a memory he has from Nice. "When I was with Joy at the café, she said she couldn't stay because someone was watching her. Gaffney said that he gave Joy permission to meet me in Nice, and he answered, 'Yes,' when I asked if he had an agent watching her. If that's the case, Joy should have expected that there'd be eyes on her. She wouldn't have been worried about one of FICA's people having her under surveillance. She must have picked up a second tail and sensed it."

"Bettke," everyone says in unison.

Fred pipes in. "There's only one reason Roni would send a private dick to Nice—she knew, or she suspected, that Joy was still alive." Fred addresses John. "Did you give her any reason to think that's why you went to the N on your reunion list?"

John shakes his head. "That is a negative. I invited Roni to come with me to Nice. It wouldn't make any sense for me to invite her if I knew Joy was going to be there."

Annie pushes in, "What doesn't make sense is that you'd invited her on a sex reunion that you planned with another woman. I'll hold my, duh, in a show of respect, Dad, but really."

"Not feeling the respect, Annie."

"Well, duh."

"Why didn't Roni go to Nice, then?" Steve laughs.

"I gave her an ultimatum about our relationship."

"Well, **that's** the kiss of death for you and Roni," the ex-husband laughs.

John actually finds himself laughing along with Fred.

I need you to do something.

Roni leaves Logan International Airport in a black BMW rental. She sets her GPS to Farm Road, Mayflower, and sets her thoughts to the last time she saw Joy Ann Watts. It was the previous year in August. **4747 Rainier Street. 8 PM.** She knew the text was from Joy, though she found it odd since the spy was supposed to be in Madrid with John Maxwell on one of their alphabetical reunions. Instead, the FICA Special Agent arranged a meeting with the DEA Special Agent at a high-end eatery located on Elliott Bay. In years past, meetings between the two women were carefully orchestrated and extremely private—this meeting was impromptu and taking place in a public setting. "Something's up," Roni whispered. "Something big is up," she said a little louder when her friend approached. "It's good to see you, Joy. I like the red hair—now tell me what the hell is going on."

"I don't have much time so I'm going to cut to the chase. Hector dragged me into a game. I have to unmask him by October 13 or he kills me and then he kills John."

"Hector sent you on a fool's errand, Joy. The FBI and DEA have been looking for him for years. What makes you think you can beat him at his own game?"

"I'm off the grid for the month of August. I'll stay off until I find him or he kills me. Every minute of every day during that time will be a focused hunt for the cybermenace. If I don't succeed and he kills me, I need you to do something."

"Name it."

"I gave Gaffney three letters: one for John, one for Tess, and one for you."

"Gaffney knows about us, that we broke protocol?"

"He knows we met at Quantico. He knows that I have no one in my life, other than John. I told him that I had a final request, and that I thought you'd honor it. I instructed him to give the letters to you if I am killed. If you don't hear from me after today, and Gaffney gives you those letters—it means that I am dead. If Gaffney does not give you those letters—it means that I am alive."

For nearly a year Roni has waited for delivery of those letters. She spent hours turning every scenario around in her head, and voiced her questions to the dead of night... "Are the letters lost? Were they destroyed? Were they held back for security reasons? Does Gaffney question Joy's death? Does Gaffney know Joy is alive? Is – Joy – Alive?"

Twenty miles from Mayflower, GPS pulls Roni from her ruminating about Joy, and sets her on thoughts about John.

Netti

John Maxwell's eyes focus on a Mediterranean city on the alphabetical list he pulled from Gaffney's system. "Genoa, Italy. Cepriano Batista," he says to the room.

Four sets of eyes focus on him.

"When Joy and I were in Genoa she met the famed master jewel thief, Cepriano Batista. They took quite a liking to one another. If she could get to Cepriano, he would help her."

"There's a famous fountain in Genoa, right?" Annie asks.

John and Mike answer in the affirmative.

"What's it called?"

"Piazza de Ferrari," Mike answers.

"Why?" John asks.

"Because Joy was at it a couple of days ago."

There is a mad dash to Annie's computer. There, in the light of day is boho chic Joy Ann Watts with three men.

"Annie, I knew you were good, but I had *no* idea. You are a Girl Genius," Mike enthuses.

"Yeup," She beams.

DC

FICA Agent Dan Shea bolted up straight when he saw her cyber signature flash past. "Annie Mahoney-Maxwell is in cyberland. Welcome to the depths, Girl Genius." Shea never actually saw Annie in cyberland before, but he spent hours studying the neophyte's moves after the Hector shit hit the fan. Shea backtracked the wunderkind, studied her moves, learned her signature—precisely for a moment like this.

The hunter's foot taps out nervous energy, and his pulse races as he jumps on her trail and follows her deep—all the way to Genoa, Italy, the G on the Watts-Maxwell alphabetical list. He sits back while the newbie isolates street surveillance that shows the fountain at Piazza de Ferrari, in front of which stood the preeminent cyber huntress, Joy Ann Watts, and three men. Shea picks up the phone. "Watts was in Genoa. She met up with three men who may have provided her help. Maxwell's kid found her. I'm going to follow the Girl Genius through cyberland and let her do the work for us."

Somewhere in Massachusetts
Rocco has glanced at Joy several times over the past few minutes. With each new look her way, he's noticed that she's retreated further into herself. He reaches across and touches her cheek. There is no reaction, only a pained silence. He touches her thigh and feels a slight tremor beneath his hand. "Mi amore, where are you?"

"Rocco, I can't go back."

"We will leave, Gia. I can get you out of America and set you safely somewhere."

Joy shifts in her seat toward the man she met only hours before, but to whom she feels so connected. "I can't run from the decisions I've made or hide from the people who chase me. My life is not my own until I deal with all of this. I just can't deal with all of this."

The MI6 Operative downshifts, changes lanes, and exits I-95N. He drives to the first hotel he finds, parks the magnificent Benz, and "whoomphs" out of the car. Without words, he grabs the duffle bags and valise from the trunk, goes to Joy's door, opens it, takes hold of her hand and the duffle by her feet, and directs her into the hotel. He doesn't break their silence until they settle into their suite. The man in charge leads Joy to the sofa. "Sit, Gia. I will be back."

Joy sits. She is unable to do anything else.

He returns and takes her into his arms, then to a luxurious en suite where he has prepared a bath. He sets her onto her feet, steadying her as she sways from side to side. She is hopelessly lost in thought. He runs his fingertips along her cheek trying to elicit a response. There is none. He pulls her T-shirt over her head and stops short. It is the first time he has seen her scars. "Gia, your battle wounds. They must remind you of your sacrifice for your country. A country that no longer deserves you."

Joy responds to the scrutiny of the man who has held her, been in her, but has never seen her. His study of her body is uncomfortable. She lifts both arms in an attempt to shield the marks from his view.

He traces the length of her arms, encouraging her to lower them. "No, mi amore. Come to me." He opens his arms and embraces her, traces along the painful reminders on her back, and whispers, "The bastards almost succeeded in making you Dead On Assignment." He angers inside but finishes undressing her lovingly and with desire. He helps her into the tub. "I will return." While away from the waif warrior, the MI6 Operative places a call. "We're at a hotel. We're staying the night. GPS the Benz for coordinates. Change out my car. Leave an SUV. Watch Gaffney. I don't want him or his associates anywhere near her."

Four sets of eyes.

Roni pulls her rental car next to a black Tacoma truck. "No clue who that belongs to." She identifies the other vehicles as she makes her way past. "Black F-150. Fred's here. Black Land Rover. Steve's here. Orange and black Jeep. Annie's here. Black BMW SUV. John's here." Tucked around the corner of the barn under a three-sided protective structure is a black and chrome Fat Boy Harley with a motorcycle cover lying on the ground next to it. "Not sure who *that* belongs to, but I'd sure love a ride." When she enters the barn, everyone stops and stares—it is hard not to stare at Roni Shields—the woman is exquisitely stunning. Her face captivates in an instant and her nearly 6' height, shorn black hair, light green eyes, caramel-colored skin, and off the charts sexuality renders most men and many women, speechless. Case in point, the slack jaws of the Netti Barn crew.

Roni breaks the silence. "John, we need to talk."

Four sets of eyes turn toward John.

"Whatever you need to say, Roni, say it here."

Four sets of eyes turn toward Roni.

"It's classified."

Four sets of eyes turn toward John.

"If you want to talk about dead people who aren't certifiably dead you're free to do so in front of everyone in this room. If you want to talk about us, that is a certifiably dead subject."

Four sets of eyes turn toward Roni, whose eyes flash with anger.

The Hotel

Joy closes her eyes and lets the soft hum, and warm wash from the jetted tub inch her toward sleep. This time, her dreams aren't of her imprisoned time at a medical facility, but still…

"What do we do with her?"

"We raise her."

"We've got our own to bring up, Liam. There's barely enough for our lot."

"Siobhan, she is one of our lot."

"Your brother's lot, and his wife's lot. There's family on the wife's side in the States. You could send her there. You should send her there."

"My brother is dead—his wife is dead—two uncounted casualties of the Droppin Well bombing, if ever there was. Their girl's had a tough go of it, Siobhan. Orphaned at two, and now left again by ma's death. You'll welcome her, and treat her right."

Seven-year-old, Joy Ann Watts, cried herself to sleep that night, and most others, especially the nights when Liam Watts was away from his home in County Monaghan, and off in Dublin on business. That's when Siobhan Watts set things her way in her home.

"You'll be getting what I think is right, and you'll be saying nothing to your uncle. Now down you go, and no sniveling, or else I'll be takin your doll."

Joy whispered into the ragdoll her nana made her for her first Christmas in Ireland. "It's not a dungeon, Maeve. It's not a dungeon, Maeve. It's not..." She kept her tears quiet so Siobhan wouldn't take Maeve McGinty away.

Joy wakes on a whimper, "Not that shit again." She pushes from the tub, wraps a plush white terrycloth robe around, and pads to the sitting area. The exceedingly handsome man who tended to her moments before, the one who did not return after he left the en suite, is sitting on the sofa with one arm extended across the back, the ankle of one leg resting on the knee of the other. He motions for her to join him.

"You didn't return. Is it because of my..."

"No. You slept."

"I wish I hadn't." She joins him on the couch, tucks herself against him, letting her head slide onto his lap. He tugs his T-shirt over his head, rolls it, and places it under her head to buffer her from his very hard reaction to her touch. For many minutes, Joy stares at the ceiling while Rocco finger twirls her short hair.

"Rocco, do you struggle with the deceptions that our world requires?"

"No."

"I have a daughter who has never met me. She turned fifteen last February. I wanted to call her, but I was dead."

He says nothing.

"Do you have children?"

"A son."

"You asked me why I fight to get home and what is waiting there for me."

"Sì. You said the reason may be a fantasy you conjured up in a pink and white room one night."

"My daughter Tess' room. I spent the night there, then the next day I was shot and killed. That is the powerful deception I struggle with. My beautiful, honey-blonde, blue-eyed teenage daughter thinks I am dead. There are other deceptions, too," Joy sighs and shakes her head. "They will come to light if I return."

He waits until her heart can hear his words. "Gia, I am sure your daughter grieves your loss as deeply as she will rejoice your return. If you aren't ready to give yourself to her, perhaps you should not yet ajar the door."

Bees, bugs, and flies.

Fred gathers everyone in the cave. His annoyance that his ex-wife is at Netti is obvious. They lock eyes. "You do remember that I got the East Coast in the divorce settlement, right?"

She nods.

"There must be a really big bee in your bonnet for you to end up in my territory."

"Having fun, Serp?"

"A little bit." He smiles wide.

She smiles.

He cuts to the chase. "You're here to get answers about Joy?"

"Yes."

"That's why we're here. So, unless you're willing to do a quid pro quo, Roni, I suggest you leave and let us get back to work."

"I'm **only** here about Joy." She shoots John a look.

"Okay. The minute any of us thinks you're holding back information, you're out."

She nods.

Fred claps his hands. "Okay, let's do a review. As we move through, I'm gonna tag questions and we can circle back to work them. Remember, folks, I don't like interruptions. Joy Ann Watts, aka DOA, is alive. During her brief meeting with John in Nice, she asked him to find out who unmasked her and who is after her.

When John returned to the States he was ambushed at the airport by FICA Director Gaffney who was doing a bang up impersonation of Don Corleone. He gave Special Agent Maxwell an assignment he couldn't refuse. If he refused it, his time at FICA was over. If he accepted it, his time at FICA was on life-support. Supposedly, the assignment is an investigation into who unmasked DOA. According to Gaffney, agents are at risk until this question is answered..."

"That's fucking bullshit." Steve barks his interruption.

"What bug crawled up your ass, Detective Phelps?"

"The bullshit bug. I know you hate to be interrupted, Fred, but I need to state the obvious—undercover agents are always at risk of being outed. Gaffney served up a whole plate of crap when he said that agents are at risk until John finds out who unmasked DOA. The unmasking of a covert, Dead On Assignment Special Agent has no bearing on, or conceivable link to, the outing of a bunch of run-of-the-mill FICA agents. We could sit in this cave for a year and not be able to count the number of governments and nefarious organizations who wanted to unmask Joy and John. We could sit here for another year and list the national security ramifications associated with the unmasking of the preeminent ones. That exercise **might** lead us to the answer of who unmasked DOA, but at this point who the fuck cares?"

The perturbed pacer takes a trip or two around the cave. He has his hand up, the signal that the detectives use when they don't want to be interrupted. "Unless..." He paces and thinks a bit more. "Unless the real reason Gaffney wants to know who unmasked DOA is self-preservation. Maybe he's feeling heat from the brass because of the whole unmasking fiasco of Watts and Maxwell. That could push him toward this bogus investigation." He pauses. He paces. He starts again. "I realize that I'm only a two-bit detective living in a little seaside community, but it seems to me that this investigation is more suited to the Federal Bureau of Investigation. You know—the governmental branch that handles investigations—the one that just happens to be housed in the same building as FICA. But instead of going that route, Gaffney is forcing the most covert agent in the U.S. government to handle an investigation that is way outside his wheelhouse. **That makes no fucking sense...**"

John clarifies. "I *was* the most covert agent. That status is past tense."

"Right, and since we've already discussed bees in bonnets, and bugs up the ass, let's discuss the fly in that ointment. Sam Sawyer was unmasked. Anyone who gives a shit now knows that John Maxwell is the Boy Genius of FICA—the most valuable asset at FICA. One might think Gaffney would want to up the level of protection on John—not put him out front on an investigation. Furthermore, John Maxwell's counterpart, Joy Ann Watts, was 'assassinated'. That event caused the Secret Agent Man to take an approved leave of absence that the Director refers to as time when he went AWOL. That's a serious charge. Yet, for some reason, Gaffney let his greatest asset stay away from FICA. He did nothing to get John back in line, he didn't interfere during the 'save Tess, save Annie' shit fest, and when Maxwell finally resurfaced, the Director didn't address the AWOL status. Instead, he sent his Special Agent to New York to work with the DEA on the Hector and Montoya cases—for months. That move kept the #1 ranked cyber expert out of cyberland. The diver wasn't in the depths doing whatever the fuck he does down there. Maybe that move affects national security, maybe not, but let's look at the most significant ramification of that: the 'dead' DOA couldn't make contact with the Boy Genius in the place where she is most protected—even if she wanted to…"

John jumps in, "Joy could have come here and used the last resort."

"You weren't here. You were in New York. Because that's where Gaffney wanted you to be. Another thing. Now that you're back to work at

FICA, albeit in a limited capacity, you aren't back to work in cyberland—you know, the place where FICA's preeminent cyber defender normally works. You are put front and center on an investigation that is outside your wheelhouse. This investigation shouldn't be handled by John Maxwell. Hell, an argument could be made that he shouldn't even know about it." Steve plops his ass in a chair, and puts his feet up on an ottoman. "Chew on that for a while. I'm taking a nap."

Fred laughs. "Well, that was totally enjoyable. Not sure about the rest of you, but I want a few minutes to 'chew on that' bit of rambling. The rest of you do what you want, where you want, I'm heading toward the nearest window."

You didn't know?

Fred bounds into the cave twenty minutes later. He smacks Steve's feet, "Wake-up."

"I'm awake."

"Okay. Open your eyes. I've got things."

"Don't need open eyes to listen, Fred."

"Okay, listen. Tagging on to some of what Steve said—if it's so damned important for Gaffney to find out who unmasked DOA, why didn't he put the whole damned Agency on it. Why is John alone in this search? Furthermore, DOA has been 'dead' for ten months, yet Gaffney flies to Logan on the day John returns home from vacation to squeeze him. The Director admitted that he had someone watching Joy while she was in Nice. Maybe he did. But he definitely had someone watching John. The black, hippie dude that John thought was following him to get to Joy, was actually killing two birds with one stone. Bird one: track John, and if Joy showed up, track her and take her. Bird two: continue to track John and alert Gaffney when he headed stateside."

John wants in. Fred shakes his head.

"During the FICA chat at Logan, Gaffney told John that both he and Hector had been investigated for the unmasking of DOA. He went on to say that both of them had been cleared.

Who investigated them? Who cleared them? Why isn't that person expanding the investigation, or at the very least, staying on as part of it? Furthermore, if the investigation into John was finished at the end of last year, why didn't Director Gaffney tell Special Agent Maxwell that Special Agent Watts was alive? Why was the lover of Joy, and the father of their daughter, left in the dark? That, my friends, is the only easy question to answer; it's because John would have dropped everything and searched heaven and earth for Joy. Gaffney **didn't** want him looking for her back then—but he **wants** John looking for her now. Why is that? What's changed? I don't know what the urgency is about, but I do know this—Gaffney doesn't give a rat's ass about who unmasked DOA. He only cares about finding DOA."

John really wants in. Fred shakes him off.

"When Gaffney raved to John about Joy's success at staying underground and giving his agents the slip, he tipped his hand. Gaffney hasn't known where Joy's been—furthermore, he's come up empty in his search for her. That's why he's had John under surveillance since her death. He knows it's just a matter of time before Joy Ann Watts reaches out to John Maxwell. As soon as John made arrangements to go to Nice, Gaffney put his plan in motion—get someone to France to follow John, and if Joy showed up, just kidnap the fuck out of her."

John jumps in. "If kidnapping was the plan, then someone fucked up BIG. If Joy had been taken before she made it to the café, I still wouldn't know she's alive. But once I did know, Gaffney had to make sure I didn't search for her. That's why he met me at Logan. He had to get me in line, so he threatened my employment. He had to keep me distracted, so he gave me a bogus investigation."

The team sits in reflection for several minutes. Fred claps his hands, and starts pulling a new thread. "Okay, now for Roni and John."

The female part of that duo shifts uncomfortably in her seat.

The male part of that duo gets off his chair with a, "For fuck's sake."

Fred takes a breather, then smiles wide at the distressing duo. "Gaffney put John at the top of the 'who unmasked DOA suspect list' and had him investigated and surveilled. Supposedly, John was cleared as a suspect. Roni, you are now at the top of the suspect list. You have been under surveillance for months and probably still are."

Roni gasps.

"You didn't know?"

"Not a clue. Are you sure Gaffney has someone surveilling me? He could be lying about that, too?"

"We'll circle back to that question. A thread just came loose, and I want to pull it a bit. Let's circle back to Joy's statement to John that she was being watched. She probably thought her tail was one of Gaffney's people. She might not have known that she had two sets of eyes on her—she certainly didn't know one of her tails was a PI named Bill Bettke from Seattle."

Five sets of eyes turn toward Roni.

"Having fun, Serp?"

"A little bit," he smiles wide. "As it turns out, that second set of eyes might have fucked Gaffney's plans. The big nut for us to crack is why does Gaffney want Joy Ann Watts? Before we start hammering away on that, I have a question. I'm warning everyone up front—the answers I get better be the truth. By a show of hands, who **knew** Joy was alive?"

No one raises their hands.

"Who suspected or questioned whether Joy was alive or dead?"

Roni raises her hand.

"Why?" they all shout in unison.

I never got the letters.

Roni gets up and looks around, "For God's sakes, John, you need a damn window in this place."

Annie starts laughing. "She's turning into Fred."

Roni starts pacing.

Fred starts laughing. "She's turning into Steve."

"You're all a bunch of freaks," John snaps.

They start laughing again.

They stop when Roni starts talking. "Early August of last year I received a text that contained an address and a time. I knew the message was from Joy, which was surprising because she and John were supposed to be in Madrid on one of their reunions. It was even more surprising that she wanted to meet at a public place. She got straight to the point. She said that Hector dragged her into a game, and that she had to unmask him or he was going to kill her and then kill John. She said she was off the grid and planned on staying off until she found Hector or he killed her.

"Then she told me the real reason she wanted to meet me. She said she gave Gaffney three letters: one for John, one for Tess, and one for me. Gaffney was instructed to give the letters to me if she was killed. I had a little panic-rise thinking that Gaffney knew we broke protocol, but Joy said she told him we met at Quantico, and she thought I might honor a dying woman's last request. All of this bothered me, but I put it aside and focused on what Joy wanted and needed. She said, and I'm quoting this next part: 'If you don't hear from me after today, and Gaffney gives you those letters—it means that I am dead. If Gaffney does not give you those letters—it means that I am alive'."

Roni starts pacing the room again. "I never got the letters. It makes sense now because we know Joy is alive, but it bothered the hell out of me. With everything that's been said today, I understand why I didn't get the letters—Joy isn't dead. But what I don't understand is why Gaffney didn't give me the letters. Wouldn't it have benefited him to make me **think** that Joy is dead—to remove any doubt of that? If he is involved in some sort of nefarious activity regarding Joy Ann Watts—it would have been better for him to make all of us believe that she was dead. Giving me those letters would have proved that point—at least by Joy's standards."

"Unless…" the ex-husband starts.

"Unless Joy gave Gaffney the letters as some sort of a test," the ex-wife finishes.

Fred nods. "Tell us more, Roni."

She takes a thinking pace or two around the cave. "I initially thought that Joy was dead. I came up with a bunch of reasons why I didn't get the letters: red tape, they were lost, there was a legal glitch, and so on. When John made plans to go to Nice, I started wondering in earnest if Joy was still alive and if John knew it. And if he knew it, then Gaffney knew it, ergo, no letters." She pauses and addresses Fred. "This still doesn't add up. If Gaffney is a villain in all this, he totally fucked up by **not** giving me Joy's letters. The absence of those letters made me question what really happened to Joy Ann Watts. Care to explain the thinking of Roland Gaffney? Because I'm at a loss."

"I don't know off the top of my head why he didn't give you the letters. You're right, though, if you had gotten them, it would have put the final nail in the coffin of Joy Ann Watts." He stops and turns to John, "By the way, we need to find out who's in Joy's coffin, and buried at Mayflower-Falls Cemetery."

"Oh, for fuck's sake, Fred."

Fred laughs then continues. "Gaffney didn't have medically trained agents at Netti Barn to help Joy—he had them there to take Joy. And he didn't allow Joy to leave the secure medical facility—she escaped. Maybe the reason you didn't get the letters is because Gaffney thinks you and Joy are in communication and that you already know she's alive. He can't give you letters from a woman you know isn't dead. Maybe that's the real reason Gaffney wants John to cozy up to you.

Maybe that's why he thinks you cozied up to him."

Mike, who has remained silent, puts in a few choice words. "Joy came out of hiding long enough to prove to John that she is alive, but not long enough to tell him anything. Joy must know that the people working for Gaffney aren't agents; they are trained operatives working with or for whoever wants Joy, or more likely, whoever wants DOA."

"Yeup. Which begs the question: Who is Roland Gaffney working for?"

Fred looks over at his partner who is sitting by the fire with his feet up, "Detective Phelps, maybe you could tell us what's taking up your headspace. And, if there isn't anything banging in there, how about you circle back to Roni's question about why Gaffney has her under surveillance."

"Well, Special Agent Shields, most of my answer depends on the timeframe. The deceitful director had you and John under surveillance in NY to build an evidentiary file. I'll let my partner explain that later. When John got back from Nice, Gaffney ordered him to get with you, so he could get information from you. It's the whole 'kill two birds with one stone' tactic my partner referred to. If John's busy diddling the DEA Agent then he's not finding the FICA Agent. Add to that nugget the fact that Gaffney gets tons of Shields and Maxwell sexing evidence for the file he's building on the two of you. Again, I'll let my partner explain that."

I do not trust Gaffney.

Joy falls asleep with her head on Rocco's lap. After many minutes, he gently lifts her head and places it onto the couch. He steps into the bedroom and makes a call. "Has everything been taken care of? Good. The woman and I will stay the night. We may need a plan to get her out of America. Keep your eyes glued to Gaffney. He cannot have her back." The MI6 Operative turns to find Joy standing in the doorway.

"Who were you whispering to?" Her face reddens and her arms cross over her chest.

"One of my men."

"Yes, your men. Who exactly do they work for?"

"They were trained by British Intelligence, but technically, they work for me."

"MI6 trained 'Fiancetti' men. And you are an MI6 Senior Special Operative. And I assume the British Intelligence Inspector General knows his SSO has DOA in his possession."

Rocco nods.

"I was under the impression that you were working for Cepriano Batista."

"Sì, Gia. But protecting DOA is a complex undertaking. I'm Rocco Fiancetti, but even I require assistance, especially since you are a hunted woman."

She nearly cuts him off in her eagerness for answers. "You asked your man if everything has been taken care of?"

"Sì."

"You said the woman might leave America."

"Sì. Most members of my team do not know who I am protecting. It is better that way. As for your plans, I am unsure what you will choose to do. As such, I do not know what I will need to accommodate your plans."

Joy works to connect the dots. "Senior Special Operative Fiancetti, you instructed your man to keep his eyes on Gaffney. You are referring to FICA Director, Roland Gaffney."

"Sì."

"You said Gaffney cannot have me back. Tell me why that is. I want the truth."

Rocco sits on the bed and pats the place near him.

Joy stands her ground.

"You are suspicious, Gia. That is good. It will help keep you safe. There are things you do not know, things that affect you."

"Explain them."

"You know that I am British Intelligence and that our government has benefitted from your services for a decade or more. When you were 'killed', MI6 was notified of the events that transpired at Netti Barn. We were notified by Gaffney to be precise. We believed the sad story of your untimely death—that is until there were sightings of you, or rumors of sightings. Intelligence agencies from around the globe began wondering if your death announcement was premature. Gia, your enemies, and allies are scrambling to find out if you are dead or alive. You are the most valuable intelligence asset in the world, and there is a high price on your head. If you are taken by the wrong elements, you will be forced to reveal what you know and if you live through that experience, you will be forced to work for nefarious ones. I am quite sure that you know this and that you no longer trust Roland Gaffney."

"I do not trust Gaffney."

"You are wise not to. After the rumors started surfacing that you might be alive, my government demanded that your government assure them of your death status. Gaffney gave his word, on behalf of the United States, that the mighty DOA was dead. And yet, I have held you in my arms and pleasured you."

She softens her stance.

He continues. "Roland Gaffney has taken a walk on the dark side. Not much is known at this time about who else lurks in the darkness, but there is something sinister afoot and he is at the core." Rocco pats the spot next to him again.

This time she joins him.

The smiling man puts his hand to the back of her head and pulls her for a tender kiss. "Gia, you are most definitely not dead. This pleasures me and it unsettles me. Gaffney is searching for you. He knows you were in Genoa, Italy, and received help from three men while there."

"You know this, how?"

His face lights, "I am a spy."

She smiles. He continues.

"It is only a matter of time before he identifies Cep as one of those men. My uncle will lead Gaffney to me—eventually. Rumors are that the master jewel thief's nephew is a spy. Gaffney never bothered with such triviality before, but now that you and Cep were with an unidentified man in Genoa, Gaffney will start digging," Rocco laughs heartily. "His assumption will be that Cepriano's nephew is affiliated with Agenzia Informazioni e Sicurezza Esterna, Italy's External Intelligence and Security Agency. When he finds the correct thread to pull, and sees my face on a security camera at Cristoforo Colombo Airport, he will learn that Rocco Fiancetti is, Alistair Duff, the covert British Intelligence spy, with whom Gaffney is well acquainted." The MI6 Operative remains silent as Joy processes.

"Gaffney doesn't know who Rocco Fiancetti is?"

"No. But John Maxwell does. Understatements here, Gia—John Maxwell will be displeased that you are with me. For many reasons."

Joy reads the pleasure in that statement. "You do not like John."

"No."

"And he…"

"Gia, that conversation, while it is very entertaining, is for another time—there is a pressing matter. Gaffney has put Special Agent, John Maxwell, on an investigation. The singular focus is to find out who unmasked the mighty DOA. We are not sure what the fascination is about who did or did not unmask you. In fact, we think the investigation is a ruse and Gaffney is using Maxwell to find you. Our sources say that Gaffney learned that Maxwell deceived him about something concerning you and that the preeminent defender's days at FICA are numbered. Do you know of a deceit that could make Gaffney terminate his association with an asset as valuable as John Maxwell?"

Joy begins trusting Rocco Fiancetti. *Really* trusting him.

"In 2015, John's FICA system was infiltrated by his daughter, Annie. It was a momentary lapse in security combined with a precocious Girl Genius that set dangerous wheels in motion. That infiltration allowed Hector to find me. For the next two years, the menace harassed me and tried to unmask me. That attempt was secondary to his real goal—the unmasking of Sam Sawyer. John said that Director Gaffney thought I did something to compromise myself, so FICA left me to deal with Hector on my own, and threw their resources and protection toward John. When I found out about this, I saw it as a personal and professional betrayal. Subsequent events have led me to believe that Gaffney left me out on my own so I would be vulnerable. If no one was protecting the preeminent huntress, then she would be ripe for the taking. I think Gaffney was setting me up to be taken by someone called, The Body." Joy looks for a "tell" from Rocco. She gets none—she continues.

"Hector devised a game for the two of us. There was one objective. I needed to find him within a certain timeframe, and if I failed, he would kill FICA's preeminent huntress and defender. I made a tactical mistake in assuming the cybermenace had already unmasked us. A confluence of events led Hector to Mayflower, and to our doorstep. The night before I was shot and 'killed' I struggled to process the fact that FICA considered Joy Ann Watts dispensable, and that John Maxwell, the man with whom I'd been involved for fifteen years, the man with whom I built FICA, the man with whom I had a child, did **nothing** to stop them from abandoning me. I realize he was protecting his daughter, Annie, but…"

"Si, Annie Mahoney-Maxwell. Her cyber prowess is now known to the nefarious ones."

"Yes. Annie will have many challenges with safety because of her cyber skills."

"And because of who her father is."

Joy smirks. "The fact that I learned of John's betrayal in the home of my daughter, Tess, devastated me. I had long been struggling with the choice I made in giving her to John in pursuit of my role as DOA. To learn that I gave up something so precious for a career so ruthless changed me—it broke the mighty DOA."

Rocco wraps his arm around the woman who is staking claim to his heart. After many moments he speaks. "Gia, FICA has treated the preeminent cyber huntress with contempt, as did the man you have been committed to for many years. I understand the need for John Maxwell to protect his daughter, but his abandoning you makes him no better than Gaffney. You have decisions regarding John Maxwell, mi amore, but as far as Roland Gaffney is concerned, he will never get his hands on DOA."

Gaffney's scapegoat.

Annie waves her phone back and forth in the air. "Fred, I've been recording this shitshow and uploading segments into a secure file, any problem with that?"

"Nope. Now for cracking the Gaffney nut."

John smirks, "I say we crack both of them."

The room **cracks** up.

Fred checks in with his team. "Anyone want in?"

"Yeah." Steve gets up and starts pacing.

John groans—he *really* hates the pacing.

After a few trips around the cave, the detective stops moving and faces his partner. "Fred, I think we need to look at the timeline from the day of the shooting, specifically the time before Joy came downstairs. Don't forget, the kitchen at Bullet Bungalow was in chaos, you were yelling to everyone that Officers Monopoli and Speil were injured, and Annie was taken by Hector. Joy entered the kitchen during this heightened time, and what did she do? She tried to stop you as you were heading to Netti Barn—to rescue Annie—John's daughter."

"Run it for us, Steve."

"Joy was upstairs in her daughter's bedroom, spending private time exploring the life of a child she'd never met. Yet, for some reason she went online. There was some sort of communication between Joy and Hector. Joy's take away from that interaction was that Hector planned on going into battle with John Maxwell, and that if he should die in that battle, it was expected that Joy would replace Hector as the cyber-drug-savior. Side note: We still don't know why Joy would enter into that type of agreement, but continuing on. If by chance both Hector and Joy died, Annie was next in line for the role of cybermenace for Miami drug lord, Paulo Montoya. The leverage over Annie was her teenage sister, Tess, who became a targeted kidnap victim. In the midst of Joy learning all that, she sent an email to Annie which was really a message intended for Fred. The email explained everything and asked Fred to 'save Tess, save Annie'. Then, Joy crashed her system, wrote a scavenger hunt message on the pink and white wallpaper in Tess' bedroom so Fred could find the message, and in turn, find Joy's computer, which she hid at the bungalow. When Joy finally got downstairs that morning, she tried to tell Fred something about all this before he went to Netti to save Annie."

Steve puts his hand up and paces. Everyone remains quiet. "I think she did one other thing before she came downstairs—I think she talked to Gaffney. If DOA crashed her system, Roland Gaffney would have found out *that* she did it, and he'd find out *why* she did it—

especially if he already had a plan in the works to kidnap her."

Roni shifts in her seat and releases an exasperated breath. All eyes turn her way before she even says a word. "Gaffney has his hands all over this, whatever this is. I'm hoping you super-sleuths have some idea what the hell is going on and why he dragged me into all this."

Fred gives Roni some reasons. "You're not going to like any of what we think, Roni, but here it is. You're going to be Gaffney's scapegoat when all of this goes south. You opened the door by maintaining a forbidden friendship with Joy after you left Quantico. John found evidence that Gaffney has known about you and Joy since way back then. Steve thinks that Gaffney didn't bust you guys over it because he was waiting for an opportunity to use it to his advantage. Our theory is that that breach of protocol, and your subsequent decades of deceit, will be the cornerstone of the legal case Gaffney builds against Veronica Shields as the person who unmasked DOA. Secrets and lies go a long way in a case like this, they provide ready-made suspicion, and Gaffney has a lot to throw your way." Fred pauses then offers a few possibilities.

"You **say** that you met with Joy in August when she was supposed to be in Madrid with John. You **say** that Joy told you about Hector's game. If Gaffney pins the unmasking on you, and Joy isn't around to back up your story about that meeting, then that meeting **did not** take place. Gaffney can run this a couple of ways. One: Veronica Shields found a way to neutralize the cybermenace known as Hector. Gaffney's opening statement might go something like this.

"DEA Special Agent Veronica Shields gave Hector the identity of a Dead On Assignment agent in exchange for his cessation as the cyber-drug-savior. Ending the cyber interference into Federal drug raids would have been quite the coup for the Special Agent, and it would have made her the Darling of the DEA— OR— Gaffney could go with something a bit more salacious—Veronica Shields and John Maxwell started an illicit dalliance prior to the unmasking and subsequent assassination of the covert agent known as DOA. Veronica Shields had very personal reasons for unmasking Joy Ann Watts—the removal of a romantic rival."

Fred checks his ex-wife's face. She's at her breaking point. "Roni." He wades in gently. "You've already given Gaffney the secrets and lies angle by breaking protocol with Joy. When he starts unraveling your professional climb up the DEA ladder, and highlights the promotions you would not have gotten if your brass knew that you broke protocol, you will not be the agent in good-standing that you are right now. That's just off the top of my head. I'm sure we could come up with a few other things Gaffney could use in the 'high crimes and misdemeanors' prosecution case against Veronica Shields."

Roni storms out of the cave.

Damn it all! Alistair Duff.

After a short nap, Rocco takes Joy to a small balcony off the bedroom. Their suite is on the eighth floor, faces the back of the hotel and offers an unobstructed view over a lush green tree line to a waterway in the distance. They stand for a few minutes taking in the silence and beauty of the natural landscape and the warmth of the waning sun. The Italian Stallion stands behind the waif woman, his arms wrapped tightly around her. He slides the collar of her robe off one shoulder and trails kisses, stopping only to murmur suggestions that she replace her troubled thoughts with the want of his touch. He ushers her to a cushioned chair and goes back inside. When he returns, he is carrying a tray of fruit and cheeses and a bottle of Shiraz. "I should have asked if you would partake."

Joy smiles. "I'm a sure thing, Rocco. You don't need to ply me with black grape wine to get me into bed."

"Ah, you delight me so." He hands her a glass and raises his. "Mi amore, there is no surety when it comes to sex or romance. You and I have had sexual meetings, and they have been exciting and rewarding."

She raises her glass in silent agreement. He follows suits.

"Gia, our time on the plane was to satisfy your need as a woman, and my need to pleasure you. Our time at the airport was to satisfy the James Bond in me." He winks. "And the Pussy Galore in you." He smiles wide. "This time, mi amore, I want to satisfy you in a way no other man has. I want to capture your heart, as I fear you have captured mine." Rocco drags the other balcony seat in front of Joy. When he sits, their knees touch, he leans forward and runs his hands along her thighs. "Gia, tell me what it is that you want, at this moment, in the next few days."

"I don't know what I want. I have been DOA for so long that I don't really know who I am. I got some sense when I was roaming—it was wonderful being out in the open. I felt free and in control, but I was neither of those things, Rocco. A person can't be free if they are being hunted, particularly if there is more than one evildoer."

Rocco tensed when Joy said she was hunted by more than one evildoer. "Gia, do you have any idea who has been following you, or for how long?"

"Someone has been on the hunt for me for many months. As for my time in Nice, I think I picked up the first tail the day before I met John at the café."

"And the second tail?"

"In the moments before I met him. That's when I knew I was being watched and by more than one person."

"Do you think John Maxwell put the tail on you?"

Joy answers with finality. "John did **not** know I was alive until he saw me at the café. I am 100% certain of that, although he should have known," she says wistfully. "He should have felt it. He always felt my presence before."

Rocco pushes past her sentimentality. "Gia, perhaps one of your tails was because of your intelligence work, and the other was for personal interests. If Maxwell did not put a tail on you—then who else has personal reasons for doing so?"

"The only two people I had personal relationships with are John and Roni Shields." Joy gets up, pushes past Rocco, and walks into the suite.

He follows her inside, takes her hand, and turns her so that she is facing him. "Gia, I am of a selfish man. I want your attention, unshared with the likes of John Maxwell." He wraps his hand around the tied belt of her bathrobe and pulls her body close. He works the knot free, lets the ties fall to the side, separates the long cloth, and lets the white fluffiness fall to her feet. Her nakedness is comfortable now. He smiles. "Ah, Gia, you must return my breath if I am to pleasure you." He unfastens his jeans and drops them to the floor. His desire on full display. He holds out his hand. "Mi amore, come."

Joy's eyes lock onto Rocco's erection. "From the looks of that, I most surely will."

He laughs, heartily. "I am quite sure that I have not laughed at a moment such as this. Gia, I'm afraid you are beginning to own me."

DC

Gaffney slams the report onto his desk. "Damn it all! Alistair Duff! OR Rocco Fiancetti! OR whoever the fuck he is has DOA! That means MI6 has DOA!" He storms to the whiskey-stocked bar in his office, grabs a bottle and a tumbler. He shatters the glass against a wall, takes a long pull from the bottle, dribbles half of it down his chin. He goes back to his desk, and directs his wrath at Agent Dan Shea. "Where the fuck are they?"

"We have surveillance tapes of them at the airport in Genoa. From there, they boarded a British Airways plane to Heathrow, and from there they went to Toronto. They boarded a private jet with a flight plan to Worcester Regional Airport in Massachusetts. There's no record of them landing there. Right now, they are in the wind."

"Find them and bring DOA in. Do whatever you want to Fiancetti. Use Cepriano Batista as leverage over his nephew if you have to."

Netti

While everyone takes a break, Annie hangs back in the cave keystroking like a madwoman. When the investigative team returns, the Girl Genius updates them on some interesting things she's found. "Hey, Dad, I just ran a facial-recognition program on the men at the fountain in Genoa. There's no camera angle that is useful from there, but two of the men were caught on cameras as they approached the fountain. Like you suspected, one of them was Cepriano Batista, the other man goes by the name Dieci. The third guy avoided detection on his way to the fountain, and when he was at the fountain, but he was caught by a camera as he made his way into Cristoforo Colombo Airport. Face-Rec identified that man as an MI6 Senior Special Operative named…"

"Rocco Fiancetti," John growls.

Two MFPD detectives, one DEA Special Agent, and two lawyers-to-be ask in unison, "Who's Rocco Fiancetti?"

Grazie.

FICA Director Roland Gaffney places the call that will make or break his career—maybe save or end his life. He needs Joy Ann Watts back under his control. It's bad enough that she's in the hands of British Intelligence, but if that agency fucks up and she ends up in anyone else's hands, Gaffney is a dead man. His call goes directly through to MI6 Inspector General Mick Bentley. "Mick, I want DOA back, immediately," he barks.

"Roland, you assured me many times that DOA is dead. How on earth could I get a dead woman back to you?"

"Don't fuck with me, Mick. Tell Fiancetti to bring her in. Now!"

The Inspector General laughs, mightily. "Took you a long time to connect the dots between Duff and Fiancetti, Roland. Now that you have, I am permitted to inform you that Fiancetti is on assignment. I don't expect to hear from him anytime soon." Mick Bentley disconnects the call.

The Hotel
Rocco pleasured Joy in unfamiliar ways. At times he cherished her, other times he ravished her, controlled her, dominated her, bringing her

to release by sheer will. His will. Joy wakes from a slumber of the sexually-satisfied, and reaches for her lover, only to find that she is alone in their bed.

The man who is now tethered to her sexual desire, and perhaps to her heart, emerges from the bathroom. He extends his hand. "Mi amore, join me." He opens the door to a steamy shower. She steps inside. He follows her, and positions her under the gentle spray of water, then steps toward her, pushes her gently against the wall. Water beats against his shoulders and back as he presses his full weight against her. He lifts Joy's hands above her head. "Don't move, Gia. There is something I must do." He begins touching, tracing each of Joy's scars.

She shivers at the contact. The sensation is unsettling. Some areas register his touch, others are numb to it. Some scars are tender, others sear from his attention. If Joy takes her hands from the wall above her head, he stops and waits until she puts them back. Then he begins again. When he has traced each mark on her midsection, he turns her to face the shower wall. He pains when he sees the spot where Hector's bullet tore into her body. When he palms this wound, Joy pulls into herself and drops her head.

"Gia, let me love you. All of you," Rocco whispers. The intimacy of the moment pushes the trembling woman to the other side. She accepts his touch, his exploration, his healing. With each trace of his fingers, she becomes aware of the beginning and the end of the scar. They are finite. They are not all of her, but merely a part of her.

Joy turns and takes Rocco's face in her hands and whispers, "Grazie."

He leans her against the shower wall and enters her body and her heart. When they are back in bed, the well-loved woman nestles into the crook of Rocco's shoulder. "There is something I need to tell you, something you need to know."

He kisses her head and whispers, "I already know, Gia."

His cell phone chirps on the bedside table interrupting the moment. He doesn't look at the display—he knows who the call is from. He is out of bed and stepping into his jeans before Joy even blinks. "Yes, sir, the woman is with me...I won't let Gaffney get her...How much time? Yes, sir, we are leaving in ten minutes. I'll contact our team...Yes, sir."

Joy is up and dressed before Rocco ends his call.

I prefer the Italian, Rocco.

John is pissed. John is physically shaking. John is—pacing? Expectant eyes follow him as he crosses back and forth in front of the fieldstone fireplace.

Fred has had enough. "John, we have work to do, so answer the damn question. In case you've forgotten, we asked you who Rocco Fiancetti is?"

"Fiancetti, more commonly known as Alistair Duff, is British Intelligence. Most know him as an upper crust Englishman—few know him as Senior Special Operative Rocco Fiancetti. He is cyber intelligence, but he's also the best covert operative on either side of the pond. He has been fascinated with DOA for as long as she has been in existence. The fact that he has her means that it's common knowledge in cyberland that the death of the preeminent cyber huntress was greatly exaggerated. I don't know how or why Fiancetti has Joy, but Gaffney is screwed. If he wanted her returned so she could go Dead on Assignment again for FICA then he'll be out on his ass when the higher-ups find out she is with MI6. If he wanted her for some nefarious reason, then he's a dead man. Fiancetti won't give up DOA. NOT EVER!"

John has no sooner said those words when Joy and Rocco step into the cave.

"You really should have updated your security, John."

Two detectives, one DEA Special Agent, two soon-to-be-lawyers, and one MI6 Senior Special Operative chuckle at Joy's remark.

John and Joy do not.

Joy turns to Rocco. "I should introduce you."

"No need, Gia."

The super-spy looks in the direction of each person as he addresses them, "Maxwell, it's been some time. You look well. Special Agent Veronica Shields, it is a pleasure to meet someone of your stature. Your work is admired in the U.K. Detectives Serpico and Phelps, it is also a pleasure. Your handling of the Hector and Montoya cases is chronicled in many law enforcement reports."

Annie nudges her father. "Damn, he's good."

Rocco flashes the pixie his deep dimpled smile. "Ah, you must be the Girl Genius, Annie Mahoney-Maxwell. It is a pleasure to meet the up and becoming huntress of the cyber community."

"She's not up and becoming anything, Fiancetti," John barks.

"Ah, a shame, but a beauty with brains and talent will certainly find her own way." Rocco turns toward the last member of the taskforce and surprises everyone. In their native Italian, Rocco asks, "You are Michael Monopoli, sì?"

Mike replies, "Sì." His smile makes the corners of his eyes a mess of crinkles that Annie adores.

Rocco continues. "You are also admired for your work on the Hector and Montoya crimes. It is unfortunate that your career path has diverged. How is it that Robert Frost once said about choosing the road less traveled? It can make all the difference. It will, Master Michael."

"Stop with the Italian, Fiancetti, you're from London," John jabs.

In a perfectly polished, upper crust English accent, Rocco informs. "I am Italian through and through and I find the ladies prefer it," Rocco winks at Joy. "Although I was recently told that I bear a remarkable resemblance to James Bond. And that was without my British accent," again, Rocco throws Joy at wink.

Unexpectedly, and in unison, Annie and Roni say, "I prefer the Italian Rocco."

John fumes.

Fred laughs.

Steve begins pacing.

Mike thinks about two roads diverging.

Fred hops up and claps his hands. "Okay. Now that we have the guest of honor here, let's get this party started." He crosses the room and pulls Joy into a tight embrace. "I don't have words, Joy," he kisses her temple. "Wait, yes, I do. When all of this is over, I'll tell you about your funeral and who paid for it." Fred kisses her on the cheek and grins from ear to ear.

Rocco interrupts, "My apologies, Gia, but they should know that Gaffney is bearing down on this location. He is a man with his back against the wall. He has been in contact with my boss and demanded that I turn DOA over to him. My orders are to do no such thing. I am here as a courtesy to Gia. She has something to say, after which, she will make her decision. If she chooses to stay, I will leave her in your capable hands, Detective Serpico. If she chooses to leave, I will make sure she does." Rocco turns cold eyes to John.

Fred breaks the tension. "Okay, then. So, Joy, what's new?"

She laughs big then eyes the players in the room. "Let's start with Roni."

Rocco interrupts, "Before you begin, Gia, don't stop to explain anything to me. I promise you that I know everything already."

Joy smiles. "I have no doubt, Senior Special Operative." Her smile fades when she looks at her friend. "For the past ten months I was living as a ghost. Gaffney and The Body, whoever the hell he is, knew I was alive, and they had someone hunting me, but they couldn't find me. No one could find me until I went to Nice. I picked up a tail almost immediately after arriving. I figured it was one of Gaffney's people, but then I got the sense that there was more than one tail. Rocco and I suspect that one of my hunters was there for DOA, and the other was there because of DOA. In other words, one of the tails was for professional reasons, and one was personal in nature. Since I only have two personal relationships and it was clear that John hadn't a clue I was alive, I figured the tail was yours, Roni. My immediate thought was that you suspected I survived the shooting. I spent some time last night thinking about…"

Rocco interrupts, "Not much time thinking, mi amore."

Joys smiles.

John snaps, "Oh, for fuck's sake. Let's get on with this."

Joy stares him down. "But of course, John." She turns her attention back to Roni. "As I was saying, I've thought quite a bit about this and have concluded that you had questions about my status. Perhaps you didn't receive the letters from Gaffney?"

Roni lowers and shakes her head.

Joy scoffs. "Let's recap, shall we? I **told** you that if you didn't get certifiable proof that I was dead then you should take that as proof that: I. Was. Not. Dead. Granted, the person who should have provided proof of my death turned out to be a snake in the grass, but you didn't know that. What you did know was that I **might** be dead—which also meant that I **might** be alive. Instead of coming to Nice to find out for yourself, you sent a PI to find me. After traveling halfway around the world, your investigator found me, but he didn't approach me or deliver a message of help from my best friend. He just followed me along the French Riviera. Why would he do that?" Joy stares at Roni. "This is how I answered that question. The person who hired the PI didn't care if I was alive, but she did care if I was in Nice with John."

A whoosh of air escapes Annie.

All eyes turn her way.

"Oh, I'm sorry, but that was amazing."

Rocco laughs. "Sì, Gia is amazing."

"That takes care of Roni. Now for John." Joy looks at the man who used to hold her love and her respect. She has so much to say that she doesn't know where to start. She finds a place—the only place. "You crushed me the night you told me that FICA was willing to sacrifice me to save you. My despondency wasn't because of FICA. The Agency never thought of me the way they thought of the Boy Genius. That bias started at the top, with Roland Gaffney. I dealt with it for nearly two decades. What crushed me is that I never believed you harbored those same thoughts, until you told me that you knew FICA sacrificed me and you did nothing to stop them."

Joy's eyes fill and she begins shaking. "I had a visceral reaction to hearing that. It messed with my head and brought me to the lowest point of my life. It made me…"

"…unmask yourself!" Fred finishes for her. Joy and Rocco answer, "Yes," one in English and one in Italian.

They are Tess' parents.

John flies into a rage. He storms across the cave and is blocked by Fred, Steve, and Mike. "How could you!" he demands. "We stood in that kitchen out there, and I told you if it ever came down to a choice between Hector killing me or you, it should be me. Tess never got to know you, Joy. You left our daughter without ever knowing you. You left me without the chance to beg for your forgiveness."

"Maxwell!" Rocco thunders, "That is the only outburst I will accept. Your recriminations fall on ears that do not hear. To say of your misdoings would take much hours that we do not have. You do not own one square inch of high ground. I suggest you let Gia explain herself."

The room settles. Joy begins. "You fractured me into a million pieces that night, John. I'd been hunted for two years by a cybermaniac who put a death threat on our heads and a time limit for me to achieve something that no one had been able to do for years—unmask Hector. I was also dealing with the consequences of giving up Tess. When I came to Mayflower and saw the wonderful people in her life, I was grateful, and I was jealous. Spending that night in her room reinforced the mistakes I'd made. I realized in those lonely hours that I didn't matter—to my employer—to my country—to my lover—or to my daughter. At that moment, I didn't matter to anyone." Joy turns to Fred and locks eyes with his. "I started to tell you something that morning before you ran out to Netti Barn. I would like to finish."

Fred crosses the room and takes Joy's hand. "I'm listening. I won't leave until you are done." He wipes away a single tear that's found her cheek.

"I contacted Hector. He had just unmasked John and was going to kill him. I told him that I would unmask myself to him, tell him who I was, where I came from, all of it. I tried to lure him with the idea that he could live in infamy as the cyber genius who unmasked the preeminent huntress and preeminent defender of cyberland. He agreed. Once again, I made a tactical error. When Hector and I finished our conversation—when he knew everything about me—he immediately put dangerous wheels in motion. He contacted Paulo Montoya, the drug lord that had benefitted most from Hector's cyber work. He told Montoya that he was going into battle with his nemesis, and like Hector of Troy he had a premonition that he would not survive." A shiver runs Joy as she relives the moments that changed her life—the moments that almost ended it. She shakes it off and continues.

"After his talk with Montoya, Hector contacted me again and told me what the drug lord had in store for all of us. In the event that Hector was killed, Montoya demanded that I be designated as Hector's replacement. If I were also killed then Montoya planned to take the Girl Genius as the new cyber-drug-savior. The leverage Montoya planned to use against Annie, was my daughter, Tess. He planned to kidnap and torture her—" Joy's words get caught on a sob, "I tried to convince Hector to take his victory in unmasking us and to leave it there. I offered to surrender myself to him, so he could avoid a death match with John, and continue his work for the drug lord. He refused. I offered to turn myself over to Montoya. He refused. He wanted to hunt me, then kill me."

Joy turns to John. "Hector was no longer interested in killing you. He knew that Annie and Tess being in the hands of the drug cartel would kill you in far worse ways—to him, that was more satisfying. Your fate was going to be a long, protracted death of not knowing what was happening to your daughters. I wasn't supposed to go to Netti Barn that morning. Hector wanted to battle you, and if he survived, he wanted to hunt me..."

"Then why did you go?" a visibly shaken John asks.

"Because Kitt was going. She wouldn't take no for an answer, and I knew that if she went alone, Hector would kill her."

Annie gasps. "That's why Hector asked me who DOA was. When he had me pressed against him at the loft window, he spotted two women in the crowd. He pointed his weapon toward them and demanded, 'Which one is DOA?' I refused to say anything. He said, 'Fine, I'll kill them both.' He raised his rifle and pointed it at Mom. You pushed her out of the way, and…" The emoting young woman pushes through and asks, "Why did you protect my mother **and** my father?"

"Because they are Tess' parents and she loves them."

It's about Gaffney.

Joy's words land like a bomb with shrapnel flying everywhere. She walks to John. "I am leaving with Rocco. After a while, you and I will decide how and when we tell Tess that I am alive. I would like to have a relationship with her, but it will be her decision. You will not try to influence her one way or the other." Joy turns toward the only friend she has ever had. "Roni, consider me dead, and don't wait for Gaffney's letters to confirm it." Joy approaches Fred and Steve. "Thank you for everything you did to save Tess and save Annie. Somehow, I will keep in touch with you, Detectives. Fred, please tell Kitt thank you for everything she has done for Tess and for letting me stay in my daughter's room that night. It changed everything for me." She walks to the youngest people in the room. "Annie and Mike, the first time you lie to one another, it is the end of your relationship." She takes a final look at the people who have become the singular focus of her life, then continues.

"There is one last thing I need to say before I go. It's about Gaffney."

Everyone takes their seats.

"I called Gaffney after I unmasked myself. He instructed me to crash my system. The plan was that he would announce that I'd gone rogue and defected FICA. He told me there would be agents in Mayflower that morning that would take me. I thought that meant that they would take me away from Mayflower and I would live the rest of my life underground. When he 'rescued' me from near death, he kept me at a secure medical facility. There was a doctor assigned to me 24/7. He was armed, and I think he sedated me at will. One day, the drugs stopped, and there was a concerted effort to get me healthy physically and mentally. I was put through bootcamp-type training. It was intense, and it worked. I was in the best physical, and mental state that I'd been in in years.

"One night I overheard Dr. Bennett say that The Body wanted the huntress moved within the next few days. I had been lying in a hospital bed for months. For all of those days, I would wake and find the doctor standing at the window. One morning, he was standing at my bedside unaware of my awakening state. He was getting ready to inject me with a sedative when I grabbed his hand and turned it on him, and after a struggle, he was injected with the sedative. When he was out cold, I ran my ass off. I'm going to continue running until I learn who is after me and why. I don't know what Gaffney's or The Body's plans are for me, but I do know that they aren't going to put them into play. I'm making my own plans from now on, and I'm leaving with Rocco…"

Before Joy finishes her sentence Rocco's cell rings. He takes the call outside of the cave. When he returns, he brings with him a heightened edge. "Gia, we need to leave. Gaffney's men are very near."

He turns to John. "Maxwell, my boss tells me that your government is ready to make a move against Gaffney. You have the information to end his reign over FICA. Do what you can to get retribution for what he has done to his two finest cyber assets." He addresses the room. "Gaffney knows what vehicle I arrived in…"

Fred, Steve, and Annie jump up and hold out their key rings. "Here," they say in unison.

Rocco laughs. "I was hoping to take the Harley."

Seven sets of eyes turn to Mike.

He tosses Rocco the keys. "Your best route out of this mess, Rocco, is to take the road less traveled," he says in Italian.

Annie growls low, "You're gonna do a little more Italian tonight, Signore Monopoli."

Mike smiles wide.

John groans deep.

Rocco laughs big.

I do.

"…and do you, Rocco Fiancetti, take Joy Ann Watts to be your lawfully wedded wife?"
"Si."

The End

More to come …

Please enjoy the teaser for my next book in the series,
They Hide …

THEY HIDE

THE ASSOCIATE

--- PULLING THREADS ---

Book Five

SHERYLL O'BRIEN

There's some jockeying.
August

"You are going to take the hit, Roland."

Gaffney took a long pull of whiskey, too long a pull. He coughed up a bit of the amber liquor, wiped it away on the sleeve of his suit jacket, then greedily pulled another.

The man who brought the $500 dollar bottle shook his head at the wasteful display. "You will be removed from service at FICA within the next day or so. You will be escorted from J. Edgar and placed under house confinement."

"No arrest?"

"In due time. The Agency wants to keep this quiet. They have what they need to charge you with treason…"

"Maxwell testified?"

"And others."

Gaffney got up, made his way to his bar, grabbed a tumbler, and filled it to the brim. "Do you want one?"

The Body shook his head, then barely missed having it hit by the bottle that whizzed past and smashed against the far wall. He shook his head, again. "What a waste. Your replacement has been chosen."

"Remington?"

He nodded. "She isn't pliable like you, and most assuredly will not be joining The Realm, but she will be on the inside of the Agency, and she will be easy to surveil and monitor."

Gaffney drained his drink in short order, welcomed the push of bravado. "What makes you think I'll go quietly?"

The Body laughed, "Don't waste your time or mine, Roland. You will keep your mouth shut, you'll sit your ass in solitary for two years, then you'll get a Presidential pardon."

"**If** your man gets into the Oval."

"He will."

"And my leadership position in The Realm?"

"There's some jockeying."

"That didn't take long."

"When opportunity knocks, Roland."

"My family…"

"Will be taken care of—one way or the other. You keep your mouth shut, they live. You talk, they die. If the latter is the course of things, I will let you live long enough to feel the pain of their passing, then you will be eliminated." **The Body opened the door to leave,** "The Realm appreciates your service."

ABOUT THE AUTHOR

She is not dead.

Sheryll O'Brien crafts characters without constraints. She tells them who they are, then let's them show her better versions of themselves. She gives them life and they live it beyond her wildest dreams.

Sheryll is a lifelong resident of Worcester, Massachusetts, where she is wife to the most supportive husband ever, and mother of two adult daughters, one who refuses to leave her home and the other who refuses to tell her where she lives. Of most significance, she is MammyGrams to the sweetest six-year-old, Hadley.

Sheryll worked several years in the fundraising community of Worcester County, writing grants for non-profit organizations. She began writing for her own pleasure after surviving brain surgery and breast cancer. Happily, for her fanbase of family and friends——she is not dead.

If you have enjoyed reading my book, I would very much appreciate you taking a few minutes to write a review and post that review on amazon.com and goodreads.com.

The opinion of readers can help prospective readers make a purchasing decision.

To learn more, please visit my website, www.pullingthreadsnovella.com and subscribe to my blog for updates on future projects.

I would absolutely love to hear from my readers, you can email me at,

pullingthreadsnovella@gmail.com